"I'm risking n

Willow said.

"I can let you look at what's in this satchel, but only as long as I'm with you. And you can never tell anyone about this or I'll be fired. I'm crossing a huge line by even sneaking this out."

"What are you talking about?" Grayson asked.

"Your meeting tonight, and other nights. At the police station. You said you go there several times a year...so you could pump them for information on an old case." She unclipped the satchel and reached inside.

He stared at her, afraid to hope, as she pulled out a thick three-ring binder.

His gaze flew to hers, his throat so tight he could barely force out the words. "Is that what I think it is?"

"It's the official case file, the murder book, the one you've never been allowed to see. It contains the details about the investigation into the murder of your wife seven years ago, and the disappearance of your infant daughter."

MURDER ON PRESCOTT MOUNTAIN

LENA DIAZ

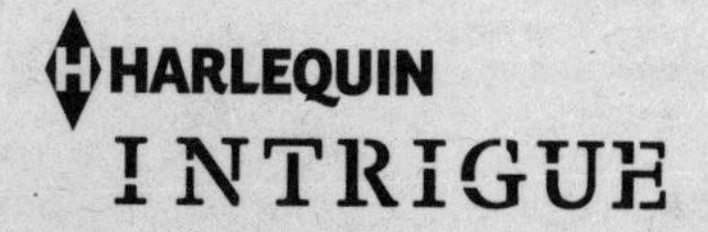

This book, and series, is dedicated to the professionals who work tirelessly to solve cold cases and provide victims' families with the answers they need and the justice they deserve.

Recycling programs for this product may not exist in your area.

ISBN-13: 978-1-335-48937-1

Murder on Prescott Mountain

This edition published by arrangement with Harlequin Books S.A.

For questions and comments about the quality of this book, please contact us at CustomerService@Harlequin.com.

Harlequin Enterprises ULC
22 Adelaide St. West, 41st Floor
Toronto, Ontario M5H 4E3, Canada
www.Harlequin.com

Printed in U.S.A.

Lena Diaz was born in Kentucky and has also lived in California, Louisiana and Florida, where she now resides with her husband and two children. Before becoming a romantic suspense author, she was a computer programmer. A Romance Writers of America Golden Heart® Award finalist, she has also won the prestigious Daphne du Maurier Award for Excellence in Mystery/Suspense. To get the latest news about Lena, please visit her website, lenadiaz.com.

Books by Lena Diaz

Harlequin Intrigue

A Tennessee Cold Case Story

Murder on Prescott Mountain

The Justice Seekers

Cowboy Under Fire
Agent Under Siege
Killer Conspiracy
Deadly Double-Cross

The Mighty McKenzies

Smoky Mountains Ranger
Smokies Special Agent
Conflicting Evidence
Undercover Rebel

Tennessee SWAT

Mountain Witness
Secret Stalker
Stranded with the Detective
SWAT Standoff

Visit the Author Profile page at Harlequin.com.

CAST OF CHARACTERS

Grayson Prescott—This former army ranger and successful businessman's last hope at solving the seven-year-old cold case of his wife's murder may be rookie detective Willow McCray.

Willow McCray—This Gatlinburg, Tennessee, detective is frustrated at her boss's lack of support. When she meets Grayson, she quits her job and helps him create a private cold case company.

Jacob Frost—The Tennessee Bureau of Investigation director may be the key to Grayson getting his cold case company off the ground and finding out the truth about the past.

Mike Jeffries—Willow's boss lets all the detectives work a serial killer case, except Willow. Does he have an ulterior motive for not wanting her on the case? What is he afraid she'll find?

Brian Nelson—Jeffries's nephew is a police officer, too. Having been rebuffed by Willow, he's now eager to take her place as detective. Because he wants the job? Or because he has something to hide?

Chad Russo—The chief of police has been stringing Grayson along for years about his family's cold case. Is he just lazy? Or is there a more sinister reason for him to have been lying all this time?

Chapter One

Grayson Prescott had been spoiling for a fight for over seven years. Tonight, he was going to get one. At least if his rusty instincts were right and the man he'd glimpsed moments earlier, skulking after a woman toward this back alley, had evil on his mind.

Not that it took much of an instinct to arrive at that conclusion.

The man was dressed in dark clothing, from the baseball cap obscuring his hair and face to the jeans and bulky hip-length jacket on a muggy night that didn't call for one. Even his dark-colored shoes helped him blend in with the shadows cast by the buildings one block back from Gatlinburg's tourist mecca, River Road.

But the most worrisome thing was that his right hand was buried deep in his pocket, possibly clutching a weapon as he slowly closed the distance between him and the oblivious woman engrossed in whatever was on her phone's screen.

Stop texting and pay attention to what's around you.

Hadn't she noticed the faded flyers still clinging to

some of the community boards around town touting the four-year-old cold case, the unsolved disappearance of Erin Speck? The single mom had left her kids with her niece and went out for groceries, never to be seen again. Equally alarming, nightly news reports warned of a potential serial rapist working this area.

He clutched his hands into fists, belatedly wishing he'd brought a gun on yet another of his useless pilgrimages downtown. It was only by chance that he'd finished another pointless meeting and had been heading toward his car when the suspicious-acting man had darted between two buildings where a woman had just gone.

Grayson had been concerned enough to follow. Once in the alley, he realized his fears were right. The man was definitely shadowing the petite curvy woman in a short skirt and high heels, probably no more than ten feet behind her. Unfortunately, Grayson was a good fifty feet behind both of them, struggling to catch up without making any noise.

If he'd been closer, he would have shouted a warning to the potential victim. But knowing human nature, he'd only startle her, make her pause, turn around. That would be all her pursuer needed to close the remaining gap between them. And Grayson would arrive seconds too late to save her from whatever mayhem was planned. Too risky. All he could do was work to close the distance as quickly and as quietly as possible. And pray.

If he even remembered how.

The woman's purse, carelessly slung over one shoulder, bounced and swayed along with her long brown hair like a beacon for the man following her. Wasn't she concerned about her safety? Maybe she was a tourist who hadn't heard about Speck's disappearance or the handful of unsolved rapes in the area. Or maybe she was a local, someone who knew Gatlinburg so well they'd grown complacent, thinking themselves immune to the dangers in their own backyard.

She must not realize the brutal lesson Grayson had learned long ago, that the potential for evil lurked around every corner. One door accidentally left unlocked, one moment of inattention could become a death sentence. Life was so fragile, a precarious, precious gift. It could end in a second, dooming the surviving loved ones to a life of devastation, a void that could never be filled.

He clenched his fists again. He was much closer now, almost close enough to actually *do* something. *Almost.* And their ragtag trio was about to pass through a particularly dark section of the street, where most of the lights over the service doors at the backs of the businesses were burned out, or no one had bothered to turn them on in the first place. It was the perfect spot for an ambush. And from the way the other man was tensing, angling his body like a predator ready to strike, he agreed.

The woman hesitated, wobbling on her high heels as if finally sensing the danger. Grayson shouted and took off running, the need for stealth gone as the other man lunged toward his prey.

A shout echoed through the alley. Long hair twirled

as the woman dodged to the side, narrowly avoiding the deadly arc of her attacker's arm. Weak moonlight glinted off metal as he raised the knife again.

Grayson made a desperate leap, arms outstretched. The woman shouted again, clawing at her purse as she fell back against the nearest building. Grayson's arms closed around the man's waist, jerking him to the side as his knife slashed toward the woman.

Hot fiery pain seared Grayson's arm, but he held on tight. The two of them fell to the ground in a flurry of flailing limbs and guttural yells. Metal flashed again. The knife bit into his other arm. Grayson swore and grabbed the man's wrist, giving it a vicious twist.

A sickening crack was followed by an agonized scream. Metal clanged and scraped as the knife skittered across the pavement.

Shouts of alarm sounded down the alley, along with the rhythmic pounding of shoes on pavement.

"Freeze, don't move. Police!" a feminine voice shouted close behind Grayson.

He jerked around in surprise. The woman he'd been trying to protect was now holding a pistol, both hands wrapped around the grip, her no-longer wobbling legs spread in a fighter's stance. A good twenty yards behind her, two uniformed policemen were running toward her. Behind them, a heavyset man in a business suit struggled to keep up. All three were pointing guns.

White-hot pain slammed into Grayson's jaw. He stumbled back, his head cracking against the side of the building. Nausea roiled in his stomach. His vision blurred. Shoving to his feet, he whirled around to face the threat he'd foolishly ignored.

No one was there.

Or at least no one he could see since the whole world was rolling and pitching around him. Staggering, he shook his head, desperately trying to clear his vision and locate his attacker.

"Freeze," the woman yelled again.

The alley came into focus. He spotted the other man in the shadows, oddly hunched and cradling one arm. He was running away. He flew around the corner and was gone.

"Go, go, go," the woman yelled. "I've got this."

Grayson turned around, his world tilting and pitching again. He drew a steadying breath, shaking his head in disgust. He couldn't believe how many mistakes he'd just made, allowing himself to get distracted, letting the bad guy get away. Apparently, it wasn't just his instincts that were rusty. If his old team could see him now, they'd be ashamed of him.

The two uniformed policemen raced past him, presumably to catch the woman's attacker.

"Police," she yelled again. "On the ground. Hands and legs outstretched."

Was she talking to him? He glanced at her in surprise, fighting the urge to retch. Slamming his head against the building had done a number on him. His pulse rushed in his ears, a blooming headache throbbing with every beat of his heart.

Pathetic, Soldier. Inexcusable.

"On the ground," she said again, her pistol aimed squarely at his chest.

He stared at her in disbelief. "You're kidding me. I was trying to help—"

"Do it. Now." Her knuckles whitened around the grip of her gun.

The man in the business suit finally reached them, his lungs bellowing with his labored breaths as he too aimed a pistol at Grayson with deadly intent. "Get down, like the lady said, arms and legs out to the side, dirtbag," he rasped.

Grayson gritted his teeth and lowered himself to the ground.

Chapter Two

Detective Willow McCray adjusted her uncomfortably short skirt, then leaned against the wall, half inside the curtained doorway to the emergency room enclosure. Inside, a female nurse was stitching up the three-inch gash on the suspect's left forearm.

Willow itched to ask him questions, the most pressing being the name of his coconspirator. But other than a heaving sigh after proclaiming his innocence earlier, he'd gone silent. The pained look he'd sent her as she'd put him in handcuffs had somehow triggered a flash of guilt. Which was ridiculous, of course. She was just doing her job, while he and the man he'd been with had been stalking her, trying to make her their victim.

Hopefully, once the suspect was at the station in an interrogation room, Detective Wagner would get a full confession from him. Willow would have loved to conduct the interview herself, or at least sit in. But she wasn't even officially assigned to the serial rapist case. As a relatively new detective, she was a glorified gopher, doing whatever the other detectives needed until she was deemed worthy enough to take a lead role. The only reason she was involved tonight was because Wagner had put out the call for volunteers, half a dozen police women to act as bait on River Road.

"He's still not talking?"

She straightened, surprised to see her boss pushing back the curtain to join her in the opening. "Sergeant Jeffries. I didn't expect to see you at the hospital."

He arched a salt-and-pepper brow. "You made a collar in the River Road Rapist case and you didn't think I'd bother to show up?"

Her face heated. "I thought you'd wait until we brought him in." She motioned toward the two uniformed officers lounging against the nurses' station counter, waiting to take custody of their suspect.

Jeffries shoved his hands in his pants pockets and rocked back on his heels. Across the room, her prisoner spoke in low tones, answering whatever questions the nurse was asking. Both of his wrists were handcuffed to the bedrails so he couldn't hurt her. The nurse must have finished stitching the first cut because she moved to the other side of the bed to begin working on the gash on his right biceps.

Jeffries stiffened beside her. "*That's* the man you arrested?"

His incredulous tone put her on alert. "Is that a problem?"

"I thought you arrested the River Road Rapist."

"One of them, yes. Apparently, they're working in tandem together. The other one got away. But we've got uniforms canvassing the area, searching for his partner."

"His partner," he scoffed, motioning for her to move with him into the hallway. Then he faced her, hands on his hips. "Don't you realize who that guy is?" He kept his voice low so it wouldn't carry, but made no attempt to hide the censure in his tone.

Her face flamed hotter even though she had no idea what she'd done wrong, in his eyes at least. "I verified his name from his driver's license—Grayson Prescott. But I haven't been able to get any other information. He's exercising his right to remain silent. And since we arrived in the ER, they've been busy treating him. CT scan first because he bumped his head. Now the nurse is stitching his injuries."

"And how did he come by these…injuries?"

"He and his partner got in each other's way."

"Explain that statement, Detective McCray."

She cleared her throat, still not sure why he was upset. "They both tried to jump me at the same time and knocked into each other. Prescott hit his head against the side of the building. The other guy had his knife out and Prescott was cut when they both fell to the ground."

He stared at her a long moment. "Did it occur to you that maybe the other guy was trying to attack you, but *this* guy—" he jerked his thumb toward the enclosure "—was trying to help you? Maybe that's how he got hurt, jumping between you and the guy with a knife?"

She blinked, images of the scuffle in the alley flooding through her mind. "I, ah, I guess it's *possible.* Things happened so fast. I just—"

"Assumed he was a rapist too?"

She raised her chin, determined not to let him shake her confidence. She knew what she'd seen. He hadn't been there. "Sir, you didn't see what happened."

"And you did? Are you sure about that?"

She frowned. "Sir?"

He let out a slow deep breath. "I've no doubt you believe your version, that both men were trying to hurt you. But considering who the guy is that you've arrested, I'm inclined to think it might have been too dark, the attack too fast for your eyewitness account to be reliable. Especially—" he motioned again toward the room where her suspect was being treated "—since this man is Grayson Prescott."

He watched her, as if waiting for some kind of bell to ring, some spark of recognition. She looked at Prescott, who was silently watching both of them now. She scanned his admittedly handsome face, tanned golden from the sun, the sharp angles and hard lines softened by a barely-there beard and mustache. Even with the slight bruise forming along his jawline, he was uncommonly attractive. He was muscular, but not overly so. Trim, fit, average height, not quite six feet tall and wearing a navy blue suit that made him look more like a CEO than a criminal. But none of that mattered. She still had no idea what Jeffries expected her to notice.

"Figured out who he is yet?" Jeffries prodded.

She tore her gaze from Prescott and looked up at her boss. "Obviously, you recognize him and know more about him than I do. So far, I only know his name."

He sighed again as if disappointed in her.

I need this job. I need this job, she reminded herself as she struggled to maintain her respectful expression. Why was it that he always found fault with her? Was it because she was a woman? Or because she was the youngest to ever make the detective squad here in Gatlinburg and he was trying to prove she wasn't ready? Or did he resent her because his boss had made the decision to hire her against Jeffries's advice? Whatever the reason, it was no secret that he expected her to fail and found fault in nearly everything she did.

"Prescott is former Special Forces," he announced. "Army ranger. A decorated hero who didn't need to work for a living and yet he chose to risk his life doing one of the toughest jobs out there. Not exactly the poster boy for a typical criminal. You said you looked at his ID. Did you notice the address?"

A typical criminal? Was there really such a thing? How many people had her boss profiled over the years with his antiquated ways of approaching law enforcement?

She cleared her throat. "His address is local, if that's what you mean. I haven't looked it up on the internet to see exactly where, but based on the zip code, it's—"

"He lives on one of the highest peaks in the Smoky Mountain range, not far from Gatlinburg," he interrupted her again. "Unofficially, folks around here call it Prescott Mountain because his family owned the whole dang thing for generations. It's only recently that Grayson sold off a few parcels to other wealthy families. Like Mason Ford, the eccentric who runs that private investigation company he calls The Justice Seekers. He built his new house there. Prescott's just as nutty as Mason and his team. Maybe more so."

Somehow, she couldn't think of the man she'd arrested as *nutty*, whatever Jeffries meant by that. "I haven't heard of Prescott, but I've heard of Ford and his company. The local news did an in-depth story on them a while back. I thought they were well-respected, that they offered protection and investigative services to people in trouble who can't get justice through normal channels."

His eyes narrowed. "You sound as if you admire them."

"No, no," she hurried to assure him. "I'm not saying that. Just telling you what I saw on TV. I don't know anything about them besides what the reporter said. But the reason they did the story was because the Seekers were given some kind of award for saving the life of former President Manning's daughter. That sounds admirable to me. Sir."

She struggled not to squirm beneath his scrutiny, already regretting the last part of her little speech. Hadn't she already learned not to poke the bear? Jeffries could, and frequently did, make her work life hell when provoked. But she couldn't keep her opinions bottled up 100 percent of the time, particularly when they were so often the exact opposite of his.

He crossed his arms, obviously not happy with her assessment. "The Justice Seekers are vigilantes, Detective McCray. There's no place for people like them in our justice system. They get in the way, make it more difficult for us to do our jobs."

"Yes, sir. Of course." She kept her tone carefully neutral. "Is Mr. Prescott one of them? A Justice Seeker?"

He stared at her, as if trying to decide whether she really agreed with him or whether she was trying to hide her true feelings.

She fought to keep her expression respectful. Jeffries wasn't one to abide by opinions that didn't support his own. He wasn't interested in alternate views or more modern ways of approaching investigations. She'd learned that the first week on the job when he'd listened to her enthusiastic ideas about steering the department toward relying more heavily on forensic techniques to help them solve cases. After he'd finished laughing, he told her she'd be much better served to focus on tried-and-true investigative tools, like fingerprints, fibers and, on rare occasions that warranted the cost, DNA. Everything else was pie in the sky, far too expensive to justify when a skilled investigator could solve a case without them.

She hadn't bothered to remind him about the growing number of cold cases in their county and the surrounding ones, knowing that would only rile him up. From that day on, she'd been careful not to bring up any of her *pie-in-the-sky* ideas again. Instead, she was counting down until his retirement—eight months and three days from now. And she was praying that whoever replaced him would be more open-minded. She couldn't imagine anyone being worse.

Hoping to steer him back to the case, instead of

his low opinion of her, she asked again, "Is Prescott a Justice Seeker?"

His neck puddled like an overfed pug as he shook his head no. "Did you not hear me say he was former Special Forces? That means he's a loner, used to working by himself. He wouldn't fit in with the team of Seekers working for Ford."

She didn't bother to correct his mistaken belief that Special Forces were lone wolves. They worked together as close-knit teams, something she knew about since her brother had been obsessed with becoming a navy SEAL when he was younger. He'd told her everything he'd researched about being in Special Forces, or at least being a SEAL. And he'd been beyond disappointed when he hadn't passed their rigorous training and was forced to choose a different path in the military.

Still, she couldn't let her boss's incorrect beliefs go *completely* unchallenged, not when they could directly impact this case. "*Maybe* Prescott isn't one to work on a team, but he *did* have a partner tonight."

To her surprise, his eyes brightened with amusement. "You're sticking with that theory, that he's tag-teaming with someone else? That he's a rapist?"

"I saw what I saw. Both he and the guy he was with tried to jump me."

"The man's swimming in money. Probably a billionaire, at the very least a millionaire. He owns a dozen highly successful companies. I swear his parents must have owned half of Tennessee. When they were killed in a car accident, their estate passed on to their two children. I imagine women jump at the chance to have sex with Grayson Prescott. He doesn't need to run on the backstreets, attacking anyone."

Eight months and three days, she reminded herself. And once again, she couldn't let his comments pass unchallenged, not when they were so blatantly offensive and completely wrong.

"Rape isn't about sex, sir. And being a rapist has everything to do with one's nature, not their wealth or status. Sexual assault is about violence and control. Maybe being wealthy gives Prescott a false sense of security, makes him think he's above the law and entitled to do anything he wants. He'd never expect the police to suspect him. Maybe that's the reason this case has dragged on so long. If his name came up in a tip in the investigation, it was probably tossed instead of being followed up."

He gave her an odd look. "I forget sometimes that you're new here."

She dug her nails into her palms. "I'm no rookie. I've been with Gatlinburg PD for six years. And I came to the team with a master's in criminology from FSU."

He chuckled.

Her nails dug deeper.

"I'm well aware of your résumé, McCray. But you only made detective a couple of months ago. And you were living in Florida when Grayson Prescott's family was in the news."

His announcement had her frowning. "The news? For what? Has he done something like this before?"

His teeth flashed in an amused grin. "You're quite the investigator. So many questions."

A chime sounded. He pulled his cell phone out of his pocket. After reading the text message on the screen, he typed his response. Once he put the phone away, he smiled again, his earlier annoyance seemingly evaporating after whatever information he'd just received.

"Detective McCray, I think this investigation might be better served if I don't say anything else about the suspect. After all, I wouldn't want to influence your opinions. I'll leave it to you to follow the leads and see what you conclude." He waved a hand in the air. "Fresh eyes and all that."

Since when had he ever cared about fresh eyes or not wanting to influence an investigation?

"I'd like you to take the lead with this particular suspect," he announced. "You can conduct the interview."

A kaleidoscope of butterflies seemed to take flight in her stomach. "You want me to be there when he's questioned?"

"Not just *be there*. Conduct the interview. You. Alone. Your first solo as a detective."

She stared at him in confusion. Either she'd lost her hearing or he'd lost his mind. This case was high profile, all over the media, the subject of daily status calls between the chief of police and the mayor. He couldn't really mean for his "rookie" detective to take the lead on the interrogation.

"Sir, isn't that Detective Wagner's call? I was only

here tonight because he was recruiting female officers to act as decoys."

"I'm not saying I'm turning the whole shebang over to you, McCray. Wagner's still the lead investigator. But you're the one responsible for catching the suspect. You've earned this. Go ahead and find out what he has to say. Unless you don't want to question him?"

"No. I mean, yes. Of course, I want to question him. That is, if you're sure Wagner would be okay with it."

"You both work for me. I'll handle Wagner. As soon as Prescott's finished being treated, escort him to the station and take care of it. I'll expect a full report in the morning."

In the *morning*? Shouldn't he want the report *tonight* on a case this high profile?

Jeffries didn't wait for her response. He headed down the hall without a backward glance.

There had to be an angle here that she wasn't seeing, a reason that he wanted her to question Prescott. Was he punishing Wagner for some imagined slight? Did he want Wagner mad at her so Jeffries could use that as grounds to fire her? No, that didn't make sense. She was still in the probationary period for her job. He didn't even have to give a reason to let her go. He just had to explain it to *his* boss. Why then? What was he up to?

The nurse joined her in the hallway. "Detective, Mr. Prescott is ready. I'll get his discharge instructions for you."

"You have the CT Scan results on his head injury?"

"Just a really bad bump. Probably knocked him a

little loopy for a bit. Understandable. But he's lucky. No concussion, no long-lasting effects aside from a bad headache. I gave him something for the pain, and he's just finished an antibiotic drip. As soon as I have the discharge papers, I'll take out the IV. Then he's all yours."

"Great, thank you."

"Yes, ma'am." She hurried past Willow to the nurses' station.

Willow motioned to the two uniformed officers, then headed into Prescott's room.

Chapter Three

Willow clutched her summarized copy of the case folder to her chest, outside the interview room where Grayson Prescott waited to be questioned. Being allowed to conduct this interview was monumental. It was what she'd been working toward for years. And she was having a hard time catching her breath, trying to hide her excitement. And her fears.

Fears that she wasn't good enough.

Fears that she'd make a mistake, that she'd somehow ruin the case.

She couldn't blame her nervousness, her doubts on her boss. Not really, even though he so often criticized her. No, the blame for her current state lay squarely with her. Because this, being a full-blown detective, was what she'd always wanted to do. She'd built it up in her mind until it had become her holy grail. And she was terrified that she wasn't worthy, that she'd do something that would destroy her life-long goals.

Even before her first day patrolling Gatlinburg's streets as a uniformed police officer, it had been her dream to become a detective. She'd wanted to solve puzzles, figure out mysteries, reunite loved ones or at least give survivors the closure that came from knowing what had happened. More than anything, she wanted to help families like those of Erin Speck.

The single mother had gone missing in broad daylight when Willow was still a patrol officer. She'd longed to work the investigation, but wasn't in a position to really do anything. Unfortunately, Erin Speck's case had gone cold long ago. But this new case—with women being beaten, some of them stabbed, all of them raped and in one instance killed—was active. It was happening right now. And Willow was finally able to do something to help, starting with her interview of one of the men she suspected of the crimes waiting in the room behind this door.

She grasped the knob, drew several more deep breaths, then pushed it open.

Prescott was still in handcuffs, attached by a length of chain to a metal loop in the center of the small table bolted to the floor. His dark gaze followed her as she pushed the door closed and then sat across from him.

She set the folder down and put her shaking hands in her lap. "Mr. Prescott, as you know, I'm Detective Willow McCray. I understand you've elected not to have a lawyer present. Is that true?"

He started to cross his arms but the chains pulled him up short. His brows formed a dark slash of annoyance as he rested his arms on the top of the table. "I prefer you call me Grayson."

"And I prefer you call me Detective McCray, Mr. Prescott."

He smiled. “Detective McCray, I’m aware of my rights. And no, I don’t want a lawyer. Not yet. I want to know what’s going on.”

In a dark alley, diving at her, he’d been intimidating. Now he was even more so. Not physically, not really. Those chains would keep him from hurting her if he was so inclined. What had her wanting to squirm in her seat like a child caught breaking some kind of rule was the force of his presence, his personality. He exuded confidence, power. Being the recipient of his laser-like focus was disconcerting, at best.

She tore her gaze from his and flipped through the folder as if searching for something. In reality, she was giving herself a few precious seconds to get her bearings again. Which had her wondering anew why Jeffries had suddenly done a one-eighty, trusting her to conduct this critically important interview.

Gatlinburg only had four detectives. In spite of its tourist population of well over a million in any given year, the permanent population barely topped four thousand. They didn’t typically have enough major crimes to warrant keeping a larger staff of detectives. Getting a spot on the small elite team had only become possible because one of the senior detectives had retired. And her master’s in criminology gave her the edge over the others who’d wanted this position—including Sergeant Mike Jeffries’s own nephew, Brian Nelson.

Right place, right time—for her. But it hadn’t exactly started her and the sergeant off on the right foot, since his boss made him hire her over Brian. She had to work twice as hard as everyone else to prove she was worthy. And that was exactly what she intended to do. She sat a little straighter, determined to work through her unwelcome case of nerves.

"For the recording," she motioned toward the camera hanging from one corner of the ceiling, "I'll advise you of your rights again." After reciting the Miranda warnings and adding the date and time, she said, "You've been arrested for assault. More charges will likely be levied, pending the outcome of this interview. We'll need a DNA sample, as well. If you refuse, we'll get a warrant."

He arched a brow. "Assault on whom? The guy who was trying to mug you?"

"Is that your defense? It was the other guy?"

"It *was* the other guy. I saw him following you and I was keeping an eye on him, catching up in case he tried anything, which he did. I didn't tackle *you*. I tackled *him*. Unfortunately, he was in the process of trying to stab you, so I can understand your confusion. Initially. But I'm quite certain your boss has informed you by now who I am, and that I'm the last person who'd hurt a woman. The assault charge is bogus. What other charges are you threatening me with? Why would you want my DNA?"

Without answering, she retrieved her carefully preselected pictures from the file, the ones that showed the most damage, the horrific trauma that had been wrought on each of the victims. One by one, she lined up the pictures taken of each woman when they were in the hospital. Bruises, cuts and haunted eyes stared back at the camera.

As she set each one down, she carefully studied his expression. His initial shock seemed to give way to empathy, then sorrow and anger as he took in the injuries inflicted on each woman. But as she placed the last picture down, the one taken in the morgue, his body stiffened and his head jerked up, as if everything had just snapped into place.

His jaw went rigid as he stared at her, his blue eyes the color of a violent storm. "I've seen her picture on TV. The River Road Rapist case? That's what this is about?" His voice was a deep rasp, dangerously soft. "You're accusing me of rape? And murder?"

"I am. Yes."

"You can't be serious."

"I wouldn't joke about something like that, Mr. Prescott."

His hands fisted on the table. A full minute passed as he seemed to struggle for control. When his gaze met hers again, the heat of anger had been replaced with the chill of contempt.

She forced herself to maintain eye contact when she really wanted to run from the room. Seeing that darkness peering out at her had goose bumps rising on her arms. Hopefully, he didn't notice.

"I saved you from being attacked in a back alley. I got punched, knocked silly and stabbed, twice. And you accuse me of this?" He swept a hand toward the pictures. When the chain rattled against the table, he swore beneath his breath.

"You didn't *save* me. I knew you were both following me, stalking me. My team warned me through the earpiece I was wearing. I was in that alley as a decoy. We had half a dozen female officers out tonight, trying to lure the man who's been attacking women for the past few months. What's the other guy's name?"

"Your team's timing sucked. You were almost killed." His voice vibrated with anger.

"I had to wait until the last minute to turn around. I had to make sure one or both of you was going to strike. Otherwise, we couldn't prove anything."

He shook his head in disgust. "You still can't prove anything. The man who attacked you got away."

"We'll find him. We locked the streets up tight when he took off. Half the force is going door-to-door."

"So a street criminal, who may or may not be the rapist you're after, is running free. And the man who was trying to help you sits in an interrogation room."

"What's his name?"

He frowned. "Who? The stranger I was trying to keep from killing you? Or the River Road Rapist? Either way, I can't help you, lady."

She pounced on his phrasing. "You say that as if you know the other guy isn't the rapist. Are you admitting *you're* the rapist? The guy on the run is, what, a mugger you stumbled across while trolling for your latest victim?"

He gave her a scathing glance but didn't answer.

She tried again. And again, using the information in the file, the pictures, asking the same questions in a dozen different ways. But he wouldn't break. He barely even spoke, except to occasionally swear or tell her again that he was only trying to protect her.

An hour into the interview, she was failing miserably. She had nothing to show for her efforts. She drew a deep breath, centering herself, trying to calm down. Then she started over from the beginning.

"Where were you when you supposedly saw the other man following me?"

"River Road. I told you that. I saw you cut between two buildings, then a moment later that guy followed you. He looked suspicious, so I went after him to see if he was up to something. My rusty instincts were right. He was definitely up to no good."

"Rusty instincts? Are you talking about your military career, in Special Forces?"

He sighed heavily.

"Why were you in town?" she tried, realizing she should have asked that from the start, instead of only covering the attack itself. "You live on Prescott Mountain, right?"

His gaze flitted back to hers. "I'm not a hermit. I do come down the mountain occasionally."

"It was late. Did you come to town for dinner? Don't you have a fancy chef in your mansion who could cook whatever you want?"

His brow arched. "Careful. Your class prejudices are showing."

Her face heated. "You don't have a cook? Or a mansion?"

"I didn't say that."

She smiled.

The side of his mouth crooked up reluctantly, seemingly acknowledging that she'd won that round. Then he straightened as if he'd suddenly come to some kind of realization. He watched her with that laser-like intensity again. "You're asking why I came to town tonight?"

"Yes."

"You really don't know?"

She frowned. "No. Why would I?"

"Wow." He shook his head, clearly bemused. "That explains a lot. I assumed, when I saw him at the hospital, that he'd told you everything. And I was baffled that he still allowed me to be brought here, and sent you to question me. I was curious what game he was playing, what game *you* were playing and what it had to do with me. Turns out, it's all about you. I'm just his pawn, for whatever reason."

"What are you talking about? You're not making sense."

"Only because he didn't tell you the truth. He sent you in here completely unprepared." He leaned toward her as far as the chains would allow. "Detective, in case you don't already know, your boss is an ass."

She hated that she was in complete agreement with a suspected rapist. "You know him, Sergeant Jeffries?"

He laughed without humor. "Know him? I've been meeting two or three times a year with him and the whole chain of command around here for seven years. You want to know why I was in town? Ask Jeffries. And while you're at it, get me a phone. I'm ready for my lawyer. We're done here."

She'd been about to demand that he explain what he meant about her boss, but the moment he said that hated word *lawyer* they really were done. The interview was over.

Her hands shook as she scooped the pictures back into the folder. "I'll get you that phone call. Give me a few minutes. Do you need to use the restroom or anything?"

He stared at her a long moment as if he wanted to say something else. But then he slowly shook his head. It was the pity in his gaze that nearly did her in. Her suspect knew more than she did about whatever was going on, about why Jeffries had sent her in here to interview him. Her boss had put her in an untenable position.

She calmly stepped from the room, shutting the door with a controlled click. After getting a uniformed officer to guard the door, she headed down the hallway toward her boss's office. The closer she got, the madder she became. As soon as she rounded the last corner and no one else was around, she took off running.

Chapter Four

Grayson let out a long slow breath and leaned back against the hard metal chair. He'd let his irritation and anger at this situation make him act like the ass he'd just accused Jeffries of being. He normally prided himself on treating people better, especially women. But after everything he'd gone through today—all for nothing, again—to have been arrested when trying to help someone had been the proverbial last straw.

And it had only gotten worse from there.

That ugly word—*rape*—had been thrown at him. After that, he'd been struggling not to shout and had barely managed that.

He was glad the detective left when she had. He'd needed the break to get himself under control, to remember what was important, his seven-year search for the truth. Being arrested was only a slight detour.

If he'd known upfront what they suspected him of, he could have put their suspicions to rest immediately. After all, he might technically live alone, but his *mansion*, as Detective McCray had called it, required a staff of people to keep it going. There were plenty who could vouch for his whereabouts on any given day.

Not to mention the security cameras around his property. After what had happened in the past, he'd been determined to make it safer for anyone working there, let alone him. All he'd have to do to prove he wasn't committing this series of attacks was pull the recordings. Proving where he was would be easy. But he'd been curious what kind of game the cops were playing.

He'd also hoped, foolishly so, to question McCray at some point and see if he could get more information from her about his seven-year quest, information the higher-ups weren't willing to share. But it hadn't taken long to realize how nervous she was and to begin wondering why Jeffries hadn't sent one of his seasoned veterans to question him. So he'd settled in to wait, more out of curiosity than anything else.

Now he just wanted out of here, to end this juvenile game, whatever it was.

An hour passed before a knock sounded on the door. As McCray stepped inside, her change in demeanor had him hesitating, instead of immediately demanding the promised phone call. Earlier, she'd been timid, unsure of herself. Now, her back was ramrod stiff, her movements confident, determined. She looked as if she were ready to do battle, or she'd just come from one.

She had a leather satchel with her, the kind people slung over their shoulders these days to replace the briefcases the older generations had used. She set it beside the chair, then sat with her hands clasped on the table, her shoulders rigid. "My apologies for keeping you waiting so long. But you'll be pleased to know that we're dropping all charges against you. And the DNA sample won't be necessary."

"Good to hear. I hope you'll explain why. When you walked out of here, you seemed far from convinced of my innocence."

"Yes, well, that was before I spoke to Jeffries. I've confirmed you were here earlier tonight meeting with him and several others, including Police Chief Russo. The same meeting you have, as you mentioned, several times a year. I also found out that they all know quite a bit about you and are confident you're not involved in the spate of attacks in our town."

He leaned back in his chair. "Somehow, I doubt their opinions alone would be enough to sway you to drop the charges if you still believe I'm guilty. Unless you're not being given a choice?"

She crossed her arms on the table, leaning slightly forward. "Correct on both counts. I've been ordered to drop all charges. But I would have done so even without them telling me to, since I now know with absolute certainty that you were not involved in the other attacks and therefore were likely doing exactly what you claimed tonight, trying to help me because you thought I was in danger."

"I'm relieved you no longer think I'm a despicable rapist and murderer. But what exactly caused your change of heart?"

"Two things. The first being that we've caught the real perpetrator. Another female police officer decoy tonight was attacked. She's fine. Her backup was there immediately and they caught the guy. He's confessing like a nun to a priest, holding nothing back. We'll have to follow up with forensics, of course, but it looks promising that he's the River Road Rapist. And after hearing about your meetings here, I confirmed that one of them was during one of the rapes, providing you with an ironclad alibi. Since the same DNA has been found in all the attacks, obviously that rules you out."

"I'm so relieved," he said dryly, still aggravated that she'd suspected him in the first place.

She tapped her hands against the table. "We also caught the guy who attacked me. As you suspected, he's a small-time criminal. He corroborated your story, had no clue who you were. And he's provided solid alibis for the other attacks. He couldn't have done them. He was in jail. So he's not part of some duo-rapist team."

"I get off by default. I feel so vindicated."

"Yes, well. For what it's worth, I *am* sorry that you were put through this."

"You said there were two things that changed your mind about me being involved. The first is that you found the real bad guy. What's the second?"

"Right and wrong, plain and simple. People in power shouldn't play with other people's lives."

He frowned. "I don't follow."

She flattened her palms on top of the table. "My boss knew, back in the emergency room, that we should have let you go. Not because of who you are, but because while he was speaking to me he got the text message about the rapist being caught. He *knew* you were innocent."

She looked up at the camera and spoke defiantly. "You never should have been put through any of this. Jeffries thought it was funny that I didn't know who you were. And since you were my first suspect interview, he let it go on when it never should have even begun. It's not right and I'm furious at him over this. Again, my sincere apologies."

He couldn't help admiring her courage in standing up to her boss if he happened to view the recording later. "Detective McCray—"

"Willow. We're way past the need for formalities now."

"I appreciate your outrage on my behalf, truly. But it's okay. I could have easily ended all of this at the hospital by calling my lawyer. You were right earlier, that I don't actually come to town all that often. It's likely my security footage at home can prove my whereabouts during most of the attacks. But, honestly, I wanted to see how this would play out too. Jeffries saw me, knew who I was. For him to not stop this, I knew something was up. First interview, huh? I'm guessing he thought I would be a good initiation for you, nothing to lose if you screwed it up since he knew I wasn't guilty."

Her face reddened. "Like you said. He's an ass."

He chuckled. "Well, don't worry about it. No big deal."

"It *is* a big deal. What Jeffries did to me is politics.

It smarts, but I'll get over it. What he did to you was just wrong."

"Let it go. I'm not mad anymore." He rattled the chains on his wrists. "If you'll just—"

"Oh. Good grief. I should have taken those off immediately." She pulled the key out of her pocket and quickly unlocked the handcuffs.

He rubbed his wrists. "Thanks. That feels a whole lot better."

"I'm sure it does. Here, your keys and phone." She pulled them out of the satchel and handed them to him. "You'll need to sign for those, saying your property was returned. Just a sec." She retrieved a form from the satchel, along with a pen. "I'll be happy to drive you to your vehicle, wherever it's parked."

After signing the form, he stood, pocketing his phone and keys. "No need. It's a short walk from the station. I hope you can enjoy the rest of your evening. Good night."

She grabbed her satchel and intercepted him at the door. "Wait. Please." She glanced at the camera before continuing. "It will make me feel better about all this if you'll let me drive you to your car. A courtesy."

"Thanks, but it's really not far." He reached for the doorknob.

She put a hand on his arm. "Grayson." Her voice was so low he could barely hear her. "Trust me. You *want* me to drive you to your car."

Puzzled by her insistence, he shrugged. It wasn't worth an argument. They didn't speak again until she pulled her aging Taurus into the parking lot off River

Road where he'd parked his car to have dinner and then meet with the police.

"Thank you, Detective."

"Willow."

"Willow. Take care." He'd just slid behind the wheel of his car when the passenger door opened and the detective got in. He gave her a questioning look. "Was there something else? Another form to sign?"

Or was this something more personal? Was she hitting on him?

She glanced around the interior, hugging the satchel to her chest. "*Nice*. I've been in Audis before, but never a two-seater sports car like this. Bet it's a dream to drive with the top down, zooming along the mountain curves. What is it?"

So it was the car she liked, not him. Not that it mattered. Even as a long-time widower, he wore his wedding ring for a reason. He hadn't moved on, probably never would. But he could still admire a woman like her. On top of being intelligent, driven and unwilling to compromise her ethics, she was petite with long wavy hair that had him itching to run his hands through it. And those curves of hers were far more appealing than the starving skinny girls that were all the fashion in his usual social circles.

"Spyder, R8. Did you have more questions for me, about your case? It's been a long day. I'd like to go home."

Her knuckles whitened on the satchel. "Actually, I have some *answers* for you."

"Answers?"

She nodded. "I'm risking my job by doing this. But I figure you deserve it. And it gives me some juvenile satisfaction doing this behind Jeffries's back. I can let you look at what's in this satchel, but only as long as I'm with you. And you can never tell anyone about this or I'll be fired. I'm crossing a huge line by even sneaking this out. I have to be careful, make sure I bring it back exactly the way it was."

"What are you talking about?"

"Your meeting tonight, and other nights. At the police station. You said you go there several times a year. Jeffries explained it was so you could pump them for information on an old case." She unclipped the satchel and reached inside.

He stared at her, afraid to hope as she pulled out a thick three-ring binder.

"Like I said, my boss was a total jerk to you tonight. To me too, not that *that's* anything new. I figure he owes you a look at this." She turned it around and held it up.

The tab on the folder had one word: *Prescott.*

His gaze flew to hers, his throat so tight he could barely force out the words. "Is that what I think it is?"

"It's the official case file, the murder book, the one you've never been allowed to see. It contains the details about the investigation into the murder of your wife seven years ago, and the disappearance of your infant daughter."

Chapter Five

Willow stood at the floor-to-ceiling bank of windows in Grayson's home office, marveling at the maze of British-style gardens spreading out beneath extravagant landscape lighting. It was a bit formal for her tastes, but beautiful just the same.

The view through the windows on the other side of the office was equally stunning. A pool that seemed more like a natural pond curved around the side of the house. Lush green, perfectly trimmed grass gave way to blankets of blue-and-white flowers that flowed like water to the tree line.

It was too dark to see the mountains, but as high as they'd driven to get here, she could well imagine the entire Smoky Mountain chain spreading out around them. No doubt the view rivaled the three-hundred-and-sixty-degree views she'd witnessed on her hikes to Clingmans Dome in the Great Smoky Mountains National Park.

The home itself was massive. She couldn't begin to guess how many square feet were contained behind its honey-colored stone walls. Seeing it as he'd raced his black sports car up the last of the mountain road to park beneath the portico had taken her breath away. And yet, he'd jumped out of the car, leading her along without even seeming to notice the beauty all around him.

What must it be like to live in a place like this and not gasp in awe every time you came home? Then again, maybe he normally did. But tonight, he'd been consumed with the need to review the murder book. He'd been desperate to see the information that had been hidden from him all these years, hoping to glean new clues about the tragedy that had taken his family.

Even now, he sat behind his L-shaped mahogany desk in the middle of the room, poring over every page, every picture, greedily soaking in each detail. He'd been doing that for the past two hours, long enough for the staff in his house to quit knocking on the door, asking whether they needed anything. Long enough for them to head down the mountain to their own homes, leaving this one entombed in silence, broken only by the occasional turning of a page that Grayson was reading.

Willow glanced toward one of the doors in the front corner of the room. She knew it was a bathroom. She even knew where the kitchen was if she got hungry, thanks to Grayson's housekeeper. She doubted he even realized his staff had spoken to her and given her a limited tour of the downstairs.

At the time, she'd taken that tour to give him privacy, even though technically she shouldn't have left him alone with the case file. But now she really wanted to go home. It was close to three in the morning and she was having trouble keeping her eyes open.

Thankfully, she didn't have to work tomorrow—or technically today. It was Saturday and she wasn't on call. And even though she didn't have her Taurus with her, she could easily call a car service to come get her. But every time she considered making that call, she'd glance across the room at Grayson, and she knew she couldn't do that to him. He'd waited seven years for access to that file. She couldn't make him stop reading until he'd finished.

Realizing she'd already made her decision, she headed into the bathroom. Unsurprisingly, she found everything she needed. After taking a new toothbrush out of a package from one of the drawers, she brushed her teeth and took care of her other needs. She tidied up, then headed back into the office.

The garden windows beckoned to her, so she chose the seating area in front of them for a much-needed nap. She set her shoes aside, then laid down on a gorgeous tapestry couch that was as big as some beds she'd seen. She tucked a throw pillow under her head and grabbed a delicate embroidered blanket off the back of the couch. It seemed too pretty to actually use. But the air-conditioning was a little chilly and she chose comfort over guilt.

She glanced around one last time at the opulence surrounding her. It truly was beautiful, stunning. And this was only the office. Still, in the short time that she'd been here, she'd become certain of one thing. She wouldn't trade places with Grayson Prescott even if she could, not if it came with that raw pain twisting his face right now.

His eyes had taken on a haunted look moments after he'd sat down and began reading. Even now, there were times when he'd scan a report, or glimpse a photo, and his face would go pale beneath his tan. The agony in his expression was almost more than she could bear. What must it be like to be him? A husband and father, seeing those details? Reliving the horror his wife had suffered. Wondering every day what had happened to their baby girl. It was beyond her ability to comprehend.

She sent up a silent prayer of thanks that she was so blessed. Her tiny little apartment, her life of penny-pinching and being budget-conscious was fine by her. Because what she had was far more valuable than all his wealth. She had a loving family—parents, sisters, brothers, countless cousins, nieces and nephews. Most of them lived one state over, near Lexington, Kentucky. She could only afford a red-eye every couple of months to visit them. But at least she *could* visit them. And she had the peace of knowing they were safe, happy and healthy.

It seemed that she'd only just closed her eyes when a bright light had her raising her arm to block it. Blinking, she realized that the bright light was the sun, its rays coming through the windows on the other side of the room. Good grief, she'd slept here all night. She pushed herself upright and glanced around. Wait, where was Grayson? He wasn't sitting at the desk anymore. And he wasn't reclining on one of the other couches either.

She jumped up and peered out a window with a view of the front portico. The driveway was empty. The Audi, gone.

Good grief, what had she done? She'd snuck the murder book out for an ongoing investigation and left it with the victims' husband and father. Then she'd fallen asleep. If Grayson went downtown to confront her boss, or the chief, about anything in the file, her career was over. She might even face prosecution for interfering with an investigation, or some other charge that Jeffries wanted to throw at her.

She whirled around and ran to the desk. Her satchel sat neatly on top. *Please be here, please be here*, she whispered over and over as she grabbed it. She flipped open the top, then started shaking. The satchel was empty.

The murder book was gone.

Chapter Six

Usually, when Grayson came here, he brought a bucket of cleaners, granite polish, wipes. And flowers, fresh-cut flowers. For Maura, he always brought the hybrid-peach roses she'd grafted herself in the greenhouse he'd had built for her and still maintained to this day. But his last visit had been only yesterday. So there was no need to clean, to polish the granite to a dull shine. And the roses in the vase attached to the square of granite on the wall were still fresh. Besides that, he'd taken a long drive first to clear his head before stopping here on the way back to the house. He didn't have any supplies with him, even if he'd needed them.

He didn't start with Maura's tomb. He always saved his visit with her for last. It was tradition. Instead, he walked down the rows of granite squares with bronze plaques that announced the names, birth dates and when each of the Prescotts had taken their last breath in this earthly realm. He ran his fingers across the raised letters and paid homage to each of his ancestors, including his parents. They'd died ten years ago, together, in a car crash. He sometimes missed his mother. He never missed his father.

Three years after his parents had passed, the world as he knew it ended. Maura was gone, along with their baby girl, Katrina.

Sometimes he wondered if there was something wrong with him, because he *hadn't* died of a broken heart after his wife was killed. How was it possible for him to function without her and without their little girl? He must not have loved them enough. And yet, he couldn't imagine loving them more. They'd been everything to him, filling the holes in his heart that his strict, distant parents had never filled. And he was still trying to figure out how to pick up the pieces of his broken life.

What had kept him going all these years were two things.

One: The hope that his little girl had been kidnapped, that she was out there somewhere, alive. He hoped she'd been placed with a loving family, desperate to adopt a child. Good people who didn't realize she'd been stolen. They would cherish her and give her a wonderful life.

And two: That the police really were doing everything they could to solve Maura's death and Katrina's disappearance. He'd been assured so many times that they were following up on every lead, reinterviewing, always seeking new clues that they firmly believed would one day result in them solving the case.

But that was a lie.

Everything they'd told him was a lie.

He paused at the granite square without any flowers, the one with the name Katrina Prescott. And a birth date. The death date was blank, an unknown. But he now knew that was wrong. He flattened his palms against the cool stone and pressed his forehead against it, closing his eyes as he remembered one of the reports he'd read in the murder book, a report written by a forensics expert involved in the investigation.

The pool of blood beneath Maura Prescott is a mixture of her blood, and that of her daughter, Katrina. Given the volume contributed by the daughter, and her age of three months, it's this expert's opinion that the infant was likely killed and the body discarded elsewhere for an unknown reason.

Grayson tightened his hands into fists. His daughter was dead, had been all this time. The police had hidden that detail from him, given him false hope.

And he had no idea why.

He drew a ragged breath and kissed his daughter's name. "I'll get you some flowers, little one. I've left your vase empty all these years. But now that I know you're in heaven, in your mother's arms, I'll bring you fresh flowers too." He pressed his palm against the polished surface, then moved to the next square, the one with peach roses stuffed to overflowing in the bronze vase.

His fingers trembled as he brushed them across his wife's name, then the ridiculously short span of time between the two dates beneath her name. Underneath that was a picture behind glass, the one her father had taken on their wedding day. He smiled, as he always did, at the look of rebellion in her eyes. Her father hadn't recognized that look, or understood it. But Grayson had.

She'd hated that her parents were so traditional, that they wouldn't let her get a tattoo or dye her hair. She'd argued that everyone in her family had the same straight black hair and brown eyes. Grayson had loved her long black hair, the beautiful slant to those mischievous brown eyes. But he'd also understood her longing to express herself.

On their honeymoon in Greece, he'd taken her to a salon where she'd had her long dark hair bleached blond and chopped off at the shoulders. And she'd gotten a butterfly tattoo on her shoulder, saying it was symbolic of her metamorphosis.

But when she'd seen her parents again, months later, her acts of rebellion weren't nearly as sweet as she'd hoped. Her mother liked her hair. Her father hated the tattoo but said it was her choice, that she was a grown woman now, a wife.

A few months later, she'd dyed her hair black again. She kept the tattoo. Every now and then, she'd chop off her hair and dye it blond, as if to relive her youthful rebellion. He never knew what color or length it would be whenever he came home from a tour of duty. The picture of her on his desk was taken during one of her blond phases. She'd given him that rebellious look he loved so much, standing at the airport in a sexy red dress before he boarded his plane for another overseas assignment. A month later, he'd received the terrible news and had flown home to bury her.

His smile faded as he traced the death date above the picture. He knew she'd been shot, that she'd bled out in the foyer. But he'd never seen the coroner's report before. The police had told him the details had to be kept secret so they could use the information to corroborate the killer's confession once they caught him.

That had always rankled, knowing they knew more about his family, and what had happened to them, than he did. He'd felt it was his right to know. That it was his duty to understand what Maura had endured in her final moments. That he should take on that burden, share the moments of her death as they'd shared their lives. Now that he had, the wound deep inside his heart was fresh all over again. It was as if they'd both died only yesterday.

He splayed his hand across her picture. Tears he didn't even know he was still capable of shedding spilled down his face.

"I didn't know," he whispered. "My God, I'm so sorry that you went through that. I should have been there, should have protected you better. I didn't know."

Great racking sobs shook him as he slid to the floor. "I'm so sorry," he whispered, his breaths ragged. "So sorry."

When his tears finally stopped, he raised his head and wiped his face. The grief he'd been living with for so long no longer churned inside him. It had transformed into a cold knot of fury against those who'd been lying to him, those who'd withheld the truth.

Those who'd said they were investigating when they weren't.

There was plenty of information in the murder book that first year after the attack. But the only entries in the six years since then were notes about his meetings with the investigators. Nothing else had been added. No new clues. No new interviews. Nothing was being done to find his wife's, *and his daughter's*, murderer.

Nothing.

He shoved to his feet and tugged his suit jacket into place. He knew what he had to do now, or at least where to start. No one was going to stand between him and the answers he needed, not this time. And he sure as hell wasn't waiting another seven years to get those answers.

Chapter Seven

Willow was a stress-cleaner. That's what her mom called it. If she was stressed, she cleaned. Right now, her little one-bedroom apartment was the cleanest it had ever been. After hiring a car service to pick her up at Grayson's estate and take her to her car this morning, her first stop had been at a store to grab fresh cleaning supplies. She'd been cleaning ever since.

Then she'd turned her attention to the second-floor landing outside both her front door and her neighbor's. Still desperate for something to occupy her mind, she'd turned to organizing her closets. But with only two in the whole place, one of them being a minuscule entryway closet, that hadn't kept her busy for long—especially when she tended to be organized anyway.

She headed into the main living area and checked the time on her phone. Three o'clock in the afternoon. Half her Saturday was gone and she still hadn't heard from Grayson, even though she'd left him a note with her phone number and address, asking him to return the murder book. She hadn't heard from her boss either, so maybe that was a sign that Grayson hadn't ratted her out and she still had a job.

Maybe.

Groaning in frustration, she plopped down on her couch and stared at her phone. This was ridiculous. She was a detective. She should be able to figure out Grayson's phone number. Unfortunately, it was unlisted. And it wasn't like she was part of an ongoing investigation where she could justify a subpoena to get it from the phone company.

His number was written in the interview notes from the River Road Rapist case. She sorely regretted not having copied it down. But she hadn't had a reason to at the time. Heading to the office to look at the case file would only raise suspicions, especially since she was off work this weekend.

It was going to be hard enough Monday morning to sneak the Prescott family murder book into the archival room. Then again, that was only a concern if she actually *got* the book back from Grayson. And he hadn't done something crazy, like call Sergeant Jeffries.

She raked her hands through her long hair, shoving it back from her face. All her life she'd been a rule-follower, not a rule-breaker. Rules existed for a reason. And those who broke them could pay a heavy price. If she came out of this with her career intact, she'd never do something like this again, that was for sure.

A knock on her door made her jump in surprise. Great. Let the weekend-pizza-and-hot-wing deliveries begin. College-boy down the hall was certainly consistent. Unfortunately, the delivery guys were just as consistent in mixing up their addresses. Their apartment numbers were the same, but one was followed by the letter *A* and one by a *B*. Why was that such a difficult concept to grasp?

She flipped the deadbolt and yanked open the door. "Apartment B is around the—" She gasped in surprise. Grayson Prescott stood in the opening, holding the answer to her prayers—the three-ring binder she'd pilfered from work.

She snatched the binder and held it in an iron-tight grip against her chest, just in case he tried to take it back. "Do you realize how terrified I've been all day after waking to find you, and this, gone?"

He leaned against the door frame, looking like a gorgeous Greek God instead of the jerk who'd nearly gotten her fired. Or maybe he *had* and she just hadn't gotten the call yet.

"My apologies," he said, not sounding all that sorry. "I should have followed your example and left a note."

"You shouldn't have stolen the murder book in the first place."

He arched a brow. "Like you did?"

She tightened her arms around the binder. "I *borrowed* it. For you."

"And I appreciate it."

"You have a funny way of showing it. Did you call Jeffries? Or Chief Russo? Please tell me you haven't gone to the police station to talk to them about anything you read."

"Not yet. But I will, after I leave here. I'm going to— Oof!"

She grabbed his arm and yanked him inside, then slammed the door shut behind him.

He stared at her, wide-eyed. "What was that about?"

She slammed the binder on top of the coffee table and put her hands on her hips. "You're trying to get me fired."

"No. I'm trying to find out, once and for all, what happened to my family."

"If that means saying anything about what's in that book—" she jabbed a finger toward it "—then, yes, you *are* trying to get me fired. What part of *you can never tell anyone about this* did you not understand last night?"

His frown turned thunderous. "What did you think I'd do after I read it? Ignore everything I found out? They've been lying to me for years."

She stared at him in surprise. "What do you mean they've been lying to you?"

It was his turn to look surprised. "You didn't read it?"

"That's a joke, right? You read it and it took hours. I literally had it in my possession for a total of thirty minutes yesterday before handing it to you. I skimmed just enough to know what the crime was. Period. When would I have read the whole thing?"

He let out an exasperated breath. "I guess I assumed you knew about the investigation. You're a Gatlinburg detective, after all."

"*Pfft*. Tell that to the people I work with. I'm pretty

sure they think I'm a gopher. I'm still in training and they haven't deemed me worthy of being assigned to a case. I'm not even sure they realize I'm supposed to be one of them, instead of a glorified assistant." She headed around the peninsula that separated the living area from the kitchen. "You want a bottled water? Cleaning makes me thirsty."

"I, um, sure." He glanced around. "This place is spotless. What do you need to clean?"

She handed him a water bottle and moved past him to plop on the couch. "I already finished the cleaning. That's why I'm thirsty." She twisted off the cap on her bottle. "Twice," she grumbled before taking a deep sip.

He gave her an odd look as if he doubted her sanity. Then he glanced around, clearly trying to figure out where to sit.

She patted the cushion beside her. "Unless you want to sit on the floor, you're sitting on the couch. There's no room for another chair in this place."

"Where do you eat?"

She pointed to the rack of TV trays to the left of the front door.

"Oh." He gingerly sat as if he thought the couch would break if he weren't careful.

"Not exactly Prescott manor, is it?"

"It's…nice. Cozy. And really clean."

She rolled her eyes. "It's cheap. That was my primary requirement when I rented it." She set her bottle of water on the coffee table and turned on the cushion to face him. "Explain your earlier statement about the police lying to you."

He set his untouched bottle of water down and braced his palms on his knees. “For one thing, I’ve been told for years that the case is still active.”

“It is. They haven’t moved it to cold-case status.”

“They might as well. The only work they ever do is put notes in the folder whenever I have a status meeting with them. In the meantime, they tell me they’re always looking at it and trying to generate new leads.”

“Okay, well, that doesn’t sound very good.”

“No. It doesn’t.”

“You said for *one* thing. Was there something else?”

His Adam’s apple bobbed in his throat. “My baby girl, Katrina. They told me she was probably kidnapped. The first few months, I kept expecting ransom calls, but none ever came. After that, they said maybe she was put on the black market, sold.” His throat worked again. “So I clung to the hope that someone had taken her in, a family desperate for a child, through an illegal adoption.”

Willow’s stomach dropped at the mention of the black market. She’d seen enough in her short career, and during her college courses, to know that was far more likely to lead to something awful instead of a loving adoption. But she wasn’t going to say that to a grieving father.

“That could be good,” she managed, careful to keep her tone neutral. “She could be really happy somewhere, with a wonderful family.”

He shot her an angry look, but it didn’t seem directed at her. It seemed more…inward.

“She wasn’t adopted,” he said. “There was a report

in the file, talking about blood found at the scene. I'd always been told there was no blood in my daughter's room, that her room seemed untouched. The assumption was that my wife was holding her when she answered the door. But I was specifically told no blood was found that matched my daughter. That report says the opposite, that so much of her blood was in the foyer she couldn't have survived."

Willow grimaced. "I'm sorry. But, seriously, take that with a grain of salt. I've seen enough blood spatter reports to know that, sadly, the conclusions aren't always accurate. Just do a quick internet search on issues with blood spatter analysis, lack of standardization and error rates, and you'll see what I mean. It's becoming the newest forensics controversy, like when the FBI admitted bite mark analysis was junk science."

"Really? I always thought the blood-stuff was unimpeachable. Like DNA."

"Don't get me started on DNA. It's not the holy grail people think it is. Again, search the internet for tertiary DNA transfer. Better yet, look specifically for Lukis Anderson. The guy was almost convicted of murder because paramedics treated him, then went to a murder scene after that and transferred Anderson's DNA to the scene. DNA has just as many potential problems as other scientific tools, maybe more. Trust me. Nothing is unimpeachable." She motioned toward the murder book. "Show me the report about the blood."

He gave her a curious look, then pulled the coffee table toward them and opened the binder. After flipping about halfway through, he pointed to the relevant passage.

Willow read the details, cringing inside again when she thought about *him* reading it. When she looked up, he was carefully watching her, as if waiting for her to tell him he'd read it wrong. *Hoping* he'd read it wrong.

She closed the binder and cleared her throat. "Okay, I agree it looks bad. And I'm really sorry about all this. I thought I was doing the right thing when I gave you this binder. Now I know why they didn't want you to see it. A father should never read details like that."

He squeezed his eyes shut a moment before leaning back against the couch. "Maybe not. But it's my right to know. And now that I do, I can work through it, accept it. One day. But what I won't accept is that someone killed them and is still out there, unpunished, and no one is doing anything about it. I want justice. And I want to know *why*."

The pain in his voice had her instinctively putting her hand on top of his.

He pulled back his hand, just far enough so that she wasn't touching him.

Her face heated with embarrassment. "Sorry. Just trying to give comfort. I can tell you're hurting."

"Nothing personal. I'm not used to being touched. It's just…it's been a long time."

She blinked. "A long time since…anyone…touched you? At all? Not even a hug?"

He crossed his arms. "My only living relative is an older sister in Arizona and her family, whom I see once a year at Christmas. And I don't exactly walk around hugging strangers." He shoved to his feet. "Look, I wanted to return the binder. I'm going to demand an audience with the police chief but I'll try to keep your name out of it."

She jumped to her feet and ran to the door, pressing her back against it. "You'll *try* to keep my name out of it?"

He stopped in front of her. "If you get fired, I'll pay you, compensation for your loss."

"Seriously? Look around you. I'm obviously not in this job hoping to strike it rich and go on a spending spree. If I thought money would make me happy, I'd go into the private sector and start my own investigation company like a million other average Joes. But becoming a Gatlinburg police detective is a true accomplishment. I've worked my butt off to *earn* this, worked for years to rise through the ranks. I'm not ready to throw it all away." She searched his gaze. "What is it, exactly, that you expect from the police chief anyway? An apology?"

He shoved his hands in his pants pockets. "I don't want empty apologies. I want results."

"You've seen the results they can give you. You think complaining one more time will change things?"

His eyes darkened. "I'll push harder this time, demand details on what they're actively doing. Get them to move forward on the case. I gave them the benefit of the doubt before. I won't do that again. I'll bug them every day until they pay attention." He motioned toward the door. "Now, if you don't mind—"

"Wait. Please. Let's talk this through. There has to

be another way. What you want is to solve your wife's murder and your daughter's alleged murder. Right? That's your goal?"

"And bring the killer to justice."

"Okay, okay. Then let's sit down and figure out the best way to do it. Getting me fired isn't the solution. And, honestly, if you stir the pot, push the same people who've been working the case all along, I don't see how that's going to get different results. Like I said, there has to be another way."

"Don't you think I know that? I've hired people, a lot of them over the years, private investigators. No one's ever gotten any traction. All I know to do now is start over, go back to the source, the police. I'm going to put pressure on the mayor—"

"How would you do that?" she asked, alarmed.

"Media. I'll talk to the press, go national."

She winced. "Yeah, that'll generate leads. Hundreds, maybe thousands."

"And that's a bad thing? It's more than we have now."

"It's a very bad thing. You can pressure the mayor, get reporters involved. But if the same people ultimately work the case, you'll just end up with months, maybe years, of them following these so-called leads your media war produces. And odds are those won't create any real progress on your case. It will just send everyone around in circles, chasing down tips that are worthless and a waste of time."

He rested a palm against the wall beside her, crowding her. "You have a better suggestion?"

Her first instinct was to shove him back and tell him to stop trying to intimidate her. But when she saw the lost look in his eyes, the pain and frustration, and realized there were dried tear tracks on his face, it nearly broke her heart. This strong, courageous warrior had given his all for his country, only to come home to an empty house and have to bury his wife. He deserved better. Unfortunately, she was at a loss as to how to help him. Her first attempt had done more harm than good, and now her career was in jeopardy.

"You've read everything in the binder," she said. "I haven't. Let me read it and see what we're up against. I'll give you a call in the morning. Then we can brainstorm where to go from here."

She moved out of the way so he could leave, fervently hoping she'd gotten through to him and that he wouldn't go to her boss.

He stepped onto the landing, then looked back at her. "You've got one hour." He pulled the door shut with a loud click.

Chapter Eight

"Well, of course, Jeffries is the lead detective on the Prescott case," Willow grumbled as she flipped another page in the binder. "Could I get any luckier?" She quickly scanned the information in front of her, then turned to the next report.

Her back ached from sitting on her couch, hunched over the coffee table. But she couldn't afford the time to stretch and walk around. Her hour would be up far too soon, and she still hadn't had an epiphany about how to move forward on this case.

"An hour, wow. Thank you so much, Mr. Generous. There are like four hundred pages in this thing and it's not exactly easy reading." She swore a few unflattering things about Grayson, then immediately felt guilty. He'd been patient for years with absolutely nothing to show for it. Could she really blame him for being fed up, for wanting to go with the nuclear option?

"But is it too much to ask that I not be in the drop zone when you release the bomb?" She *really* didn't want to lose her job. She sighed and turned the page.

From what she'd gleaned so far, the crime itself was

pretty basic. Young wife and daughter at home alone while the husband was on one of his army ranger missions out of the country. The staff that maintained the household had left for the weekend, which seemed to be the norm for the Prescotts. Willow remembered Grayson's housekeeper apologizing to her last night because she was leaving. She'd been worried that Willow might need something if she was still there on Saturday, which was why she'd given her that brief tour of the kitchen and the downstairs.

That same housekeeper, Mrs. Scott, was listed in the file as the first of the staff to arrive on that fateful Monday morning seven years ago. She'd found the front door standing open and Mrs. Prescott lying in a pool of drying blood in the foyer, clearly dead. The housekeeper hadn't even gone inside. She'd been too scared. Instead, she'd called 911 and sat in her locked car until police arrived.

They'd cleared the house, making sure no intruders were hiding anywhere. And at the housekeeper's urging, they'd searched for the Prescotts' three-month old baby girl, unsuccessfully.

And that was it. No suspects were listed. No witnesses. Maura Prescott had been shot twice—once in the chest, once in the head—and left to die. Or at least that's what was in the initial press release saved in the binder.

The coroner's report told another story.

Delicate, petite Maura had been brutally beaten and slashed several times with a knife. Even her blond hair had been hacked, with chunks of it found all over the foyer. Only then had she been shot, almost mercifully at that point. Willow wondered whether Grayson had already known about her suffering, the awful things done to her. Or had he discovered it because she'd foolishly given him the murder book?

She shook her head, adding that to her growing list of things to feel guilty about. Stupid decision. Stupid. She should have known there'd be things in the folder the police would keep from the family. It was standard operating procedure. Families didn't understand that. But police often held back details about crimes, especially ones like this.

They had to.

False confessions, unfortunately, weren't that uncommon. If an unbalanced person with a criminal record confessed to Maura's murder, the easiest way to determine if the confession warranted further investigation was whether the person knew intimate details that hadn't been released to the public. And in this case, it seemed more kindness than meanness to not have told the husband that his wife had suffered far more than just being shot.

Still, giving Grayson false hope that his daughter was alive seemed particularly cruel. Then again, Willow understood the reasoning after reading the report. It was one forensic expert's opinion that the daughter was dead. But there was a contradicting report, later in the file, that was inconclusive on that subject. Personally, Willow was betting the little girl had been killed. She knew the forensic expert who'd come to that conclusion, and he was one of the best around.

The other so-called expert wasn't even in the field anymore. He'd retired not long after that opinion was written. But there really was no way to be sure.

She picked up her phone from the coffee table and checked the time. Her stomach dropped. Grayson would be here any minute and she'd only made it halfway through the binder. Even as familiar with cop-speak as she was, and able to quickly scan various forms for the sections she knew would have the most important information, she still needed another hour, maybe two, to get through all of it.

So many pieces of paper. So few that were actually useful. Most of them were interview summaries, with the details behind each interview maintained in separate binders since they couldn't possibly all fit in this one. Family, friends, staff, neighbors—if people who lived over a mile away on the other side of Prescott Mountain could really be counted as neighbors. All had been questioned, multiple times. Not one of them had anything bad to say about the Prescotts, especially Maura. The twenty-eight-year-old wife and mother was adored by everyone who knew her.

So what had actually happened? What did it all say when taken as a whole?

A beautiful young woman had been assaulted and murdered in her own home, her daughter allegedly killed—either on purpose or by accident. No known enemies. No signs of breaking and entering, which led police to believe she either knew her attacker or had opened the door because he didn't seem threatening.

So who was he? Who would a woman living in an

isolated house with a baby girl to protect open her door to?

A cop. That was the very first thing to pop into Willow's head. The idea that she could know and work with someone capable of such a crime sent a chill down her spine. But that was one theory that Jeffries had meticulously worked on this case. Everyone in law enforcement, from Gatlinburg PD to the park rangers in the nearby Smoky Mountains National Park had been interviewed, and alibis checked. Even his nephew, Brian, who was still in the police academy at the time, had to provide an alibi, which was solid since he was with his uncle, Sergeant Jeffries during the attack. Willow would have been questioned too, if she'd been working for Gatlinburg PD back then. But that was her last year in college and she'd been living in Tallahassee attending Florida State University.

Jeffries's conclusion? It wasn't a cop.

Of course, it could have been someone posing as one. There was no way to rule it out.

What else? A delivery person? How many people would question opening their door to someone in a well-known type of delivery vehicle, as long as they were wearing a uniform? Uniforms were easy to come by, or to fake. And with online shopping so popular these days, having packages delivered to someone's home was commonplace.

Once again, she couldn't fault Jeffries on that angle. He'd performed due diligence to rule it in or out. He'd reviewed credit-card receipts to prove some orders had been made. But when he followed up, none of them had been delivered on the day of the murder. Of course, as with the cop-as-the-killer theory, it was difficult to prove a negative. Even though they couldn't prove a real delivery driver had come to the house, they couldn't prove someone posing as one hadn't been there.

The odd thing was that there was no robbery. As remote as the home was, someone could have loaded up a huge truck with valuables and taken hours to do so, and no one would have noticed. But the staff, and Grayson after he flew back home, verified that nothing was taken. No jewelry, no credit cards or cash from the victim's purse upstairs, no priceless works of art or knickknacks scattered throughout the home. So what did that leave as the perpetrator's goal?

Murder.

Then again, maybe not.

If the killer had gone there to rob the place, he might have thought no one was home. But when his quick knock on the door was actually answered, he panicked and killed the mother and the child she was holding. After the murder, he could have been too scared and shaken to go through with the original plan and ran away. Willow could see that happening, especially if the killer was young and didn't have a mile-long rap sheet behind him yet. Plausible. Possible. But basically irrelevant since it didn't help solve the case.

Chimes sounded on her phone. It was the alarm she'd set. Time was up.

She sighed and pocketed her phone. Might as well meet Grayson outside. It would give her a chance to walk around and work out the kinks in her shoulders and back.

Leaving the murder book where it was, she grabbed her keys and headed out the door.

It didn't surprise her that the second she reached the bottom step, he pulled up in that gorgeous Audi. She'd pegged him as a type-A personality, just like her. Being punctual was important to her and she generally admired the trait in others. But this one time, she would have preferred he be late, maybe a couple of hours late.

He cut the engine and got out, a living breathing poster for a Matrix movie in his black suit, crisp white shirt and dark shades. Or maybe the devastatingly handsome, much younger brother of Tommy Lee Jones in the *Men in Black* movies. Too bad he was emotionally unavailable and wanted to get her fired.

After rounding the car, he leaned back against the hood. He tugged his shades down just enough to peer at her over the top. "Since you don't look thrilled to see me, I'm guessing you weren't able to come up with a brilliant plan to light a fire under the investigation."

She cocked her head. "You're saying women are usually thrilled to see you?"

His mouth quirked. "Touché. How about it? Any ideas?"

She crossed her arms. "I need more time. Giving me only an hour isn't fair."

"Do you honestly think more time would make a difference?"

"It might."

"I said *honestly.*"

She huffed. "Maybe not. I don't know. But I'd kind of like to try before you destroy my livelihood just because I was foolish enough to want to help you in the first place."

"Ouch."

"If the Louis Vuitton fits."

He sighed heavily, then checked his watch. She couldn't remember the last time she'd seen someone even wear a watch, especially a fancy one that looked to have a compass and no telling what else. Maybe it went along with his millionaire, or billionaire, image. Or maybe he just preferred a quick glance at his wrist instead of having to dig a phone out of his pocket. She could see the merit in that. It didn't mean she'd take to wearing one though.

"Are you hungry?" he asked. "I haven't eaten all day and my stomach's burning a hole through my back."

She gave him a suspicious look. "Why do you ask?"

He looked at her over the top of his shades again. "I prefer to destroy careers on a full stomach."

"Well, if you put it that way, it sounds so appealing."

He laughed, then sobered, seemingly surprised—which had Willow feeling sad. Did he laugh so infrequently it shocked him?

"Let's have dinner," he said. "Somewhere private so we can talk. I don't want to hurt you, Willow. But I'm not letting this drop. Let's talk it through, see if we can come up with a compromise."

"Compromise? That sounds good. I like compromise."

He rounded to the passenger side of the car, opened the door and waited.

"My purse is in my apartment—"

"You don't need it. Dinner's on me."

"Well, okay." She hurried to the car, smiling up at him as she slid onto the cushy leather seat. "Make it somewhere expensive then. I love lobster."

"I know just the place."

Chapter Nine

"I absolutely can*not* go in there."

The panic in Willow's voice had Grayson glancing at her as he parked in front of the restaurant. "You wanted lobster. You can't get better lobster anywhere else in Gatlinburg."

Her eyes, which he'd only just realized were a sea green, went wide with panic as she surveyed the parking lot. "The cheapest car I see is a Hummer. They probably wouldn't even let me park my Taurus on the road out front. Good grief, look at that woman's jewelry. I need sunglasses to keep all those diamonds from blinding me." She vigorously shook her head. "No way. I can't go in there. I'm wearing jeans and a blouse. They'll think I'm the help and shoo me through the back door into the kitchen."

"No one will care. It's okay."

"You can't make me get out of this car."

"You sure about that?"

She gave him a droll look and pulled up the leg of her jeans to reveal an ankle holster. "Positive."

He rolled his eyes as she smoothed her pant leg back into place.

"Let's go somewhere else," she said.

"I thought you wanted expensive."

"I was totally teasing. Good grief, Nob Hill Seafood and Steaks? Even the name sounds pretentious. I've never even heard of this place and I've lived here for six years."

"You win. We'll go somewhere else. Anything particular in mind?"

She frowned and gave him the once-over.

He glanced down, wondering if he had a spot on his tie or something equally egregious. "What?"

"Do you even *own* a pair of jeans? Never mind. Just take us into town, somewhere full of tacky tourists. Someplace so loud no one can hear anything we talk about at our table."

"As the lady wishes."

Twenty minutes later, they were tucked into a back corner booth in a seafood place just off the main drag. As requested, it was hopping with tourists. Reruns of sports games played on TVs hanging from nearly every available spot on the ceiling that wasn't already covered by an animal head. With the clinking of dishes, loud conversations and laughter, and equally loud music pumping out of the speakers, he could understand why there was closed-captioning running along the bottom of each television. There was certainly no way anyone would be able to hear them.

After the waitress took their orders, Willow gave him the once-over again, frowning.

"What now?" he asked.

"Can you lose the jacket?"

"You're embarrassed that I'm *over*dressed?"

"Pretty much. Yeah."

Shaking his head in exasperation, he took off his jacket and set it on the bench beside him. "Do I meet your low standards now?"

"Not quite. Ditch the noose."

"Oh, for the love of..." He shook his head. "Fine. Whatever. I'll take off the tie." He loosened it and yanked it over his head and tossed it on top of his jacket. "Quit stalling. We need to discuss our options."

She sighed and crossed her forearms on top of the table. "I wish I knew some options, other than the one you seem so fond of."

He leaned back, resting one arm across the top of the booth. "How much of it did you get through?"

"The binder? Half, maybe a little more than that. Actually, I did quickly *scan* through the whole thing first, before reading in more detail. I got a good feel for what's been done and I have to say, they spent a lot of time on this case. The first year anyway. There don't seem to be any leads left to follow."

"That's not what I wanted to hear."

She shrugged. "It's true. And believe me, I hate to say it. Because I'm no fan of my boss and he's the lead detective on this. But he was wickedly detailed, and that binder is just the summary. There are other binders with even more details to back it up." She glanced at him, then held up her hands. "Uh-uh. Don't look at me like that. You're assuming the other ones will have some magic key to solving this. I'm telling you, they won't. Everything is cross-referenced in the murder book we have. If there's a thread to pull, we'd find the end of it in the murder book itself."

Her eyes widened and she looked around, as if just realizing she'd said murder book out loud.

"Don't worry. You could scream in here and no one would hear you," he told her.

She scooted over in the booth until their thighs were touching. "I'm not taking any chances. We'll be able to keep our voices lower if we're closer."

He was glad the waitress arrived with their order just then, because the warmth of Willow's soft thigh pressed against his had temporarily robbed him of the ability to speak. He kept his expression carefully blank while she chatted with the waitress and asked for extra napkins and butter.

When they were alone once again, he watched her happily breaking the shell to get at the meat and realized it truly didn't faze her that they were sitting so close, that he could feel her body heat warming his, that her elbow occasionally brushed his side. For his part, it was almost all he could think about.

Until he glanced down at the gold ring on his left hand.

He stared at it a long moment, then reached across the table for the salt and used the movement to subtly scoot over just enough so they were no longer touching. When he caught Willow's questioning glance, he realized maybe he hadn't been as subtle as he'd hoped.

"Uh, did you want some? For your baked potato?" He raised the saltshaker.

She slowly shook her head, before turning her attention to her meal.

He let out a slow breath, and silently reminded himself why he was here. This unexpected attraction to the pretty detective was unwelcome, to say the least. He'd vowed to find Maura's killer years ago, and that had to be his priority. Not some fling that would only distract him from what really mattered.

Her warm hand pressed against his forearm. He forced himself not to pull away this time and simply arched a brow in question.

"Is something wrong?" she asked. "I mean, other than the obvious?"

He blinked. "The obvious?"

She motioned with her hand in the air. "The case. Is something else bothering you? You got quiet after the food arrived."

"No, just thinking. You know, about our options, or lack of them." He dug into his lobster, hoping that focusing on his meal would re-center him. He wasn't normally this easily distracted. But from the moment they'd sat beside each other on her tiny couch he'd been off-kilter. There was something so…refreshing about her, so honest, so…fun that he'd stormed out of her apartment for self-preservation.

He'd assumed once he'd put some distance between them that things would get back to normal. But the second he'd returned, he knew he was in trouble. Somehow he had to stay focused.

On Maura.

And Katrina.

"Ready to talk?" she asked, leaning in close.

"Yes," he said, perhaps a little too enthusiastically, judging by her wide eyes. He cleared his throat. "Let's discuss your impression of the case file. Are there questions I can answer for you?"

She nodded, took a deep sip of her sweet tea, then turned in the booth to face him. "Those interviews, there were a dozen or so people questioned who worked for you at your estate. Does that sound right? I have no idea how many people it takes to run a place like that."

"Too many. But twelve-ish sounds in the ballpark. The grounds alone require half a dozen gardeners. The housekeeper has a staff of four or five. Then there's the cook, who complains I don't use his services as much as I should. I think he's about ready to quit on me."

"Is he the same cook who was working there back then?"

"They're all the same people who worked for me back then. At least the house staff is. The cook, or *chef* as he prefers to be called, has been there the longest, over thirty years. Mr. Baines, the head gardener, has been there almost as long. But I think the young people he uses for the physical labor come and go. Mainly college-aged kids earning extra money between semesters or while on summer break."

He idly traced a bead of water running down the side of his glass. "I've thought about selling, many times. It's a lot to keep up for one person. I offered it to my sister and her husband, but they don't want the place. Ashley prefers the climate in Arizona, the beauty of the desert. And she says the house reminds her too much of our parents."

She shot him a questioning glance. "Is that a bad thing?"

He considered her question. "Good and bad, I suppose. Our parents were…complicated. Life at home could be…difficult. They were extremely strict, old-school, formal." The way she was looking at him, he didn't think his vague references fooled her one bit. But instead of pressing for more information, she surprised him by smiling and flicking the collar of his dress shirt.

"And you're not? Formal?"

He scoffed. "Compared to them, no. I guess it's all relative." He cocked his head, studying her. "You and Ashley would get along great. She's the exact opposite of me." He motioned toward the boisterous tourists surrounding them. "She'd absolutely love a place like this."

She leaned in close. "Then there's hope for you yet. Maybe we can work some of that starch out of your collar before this is over."

"This?"

She motioned with her hands again. "You know. The investigation."

"Ah. Right. Somehow we keep getting off track. You were asking about the interviews. Is there anything else that struck you?"

"Not really. I mean, it's all typical Jeffries, of course."

"Typical? In what way."

"Well, kind of like you and your sister, I'm guessing. You seem to approach life in different ways. My boss and I approach cases in different ways. Or at least if he'd let me work a case the way I want to. I'd definitely do it differently than him."

"How so?"

"It's just, well, he likes to do things the tried-and-true way, kind of old-fashioned. Not that it's wrong or anything. He's into solid gumshoe work, pounding the pavement, knock-and-talks—"

"Knock-and-talks?"

"Cop-speak. It's when you canvass a neighborhood, go door-to-door. You know, knock on the door and talk to whoever's there."

"Knock-and-talk. Got it."

She wiped her mouth with her napkin and shoved her plate back. "He's thorough. He really is, as far as interviews and fingerprints, stuff like that. It's just, well, I understand we have a limited budget and all, but if it were up to me, we'd do a lot more testing on any physical evidence in each case. Heck, I'd have the forensic team collect a lot more evidence than they currently do. I'd involve TBI more—"

"TBI. Tennessee Bureau of Investigation?"

"Right. State police. They've got a terrific lab, great scientists working for them. And they're not sloppy or stupid about how they handle the testing or interpret the DNA or blood spatter data. But it's expensive, really expensive. And they get backed up for months on testing. Sometimes you can go to trial without ever having your evidence tested because the lab couldn't get to it. That leads to plea deals and negotiations because the evidence is too weak without those lab results. You bluff and threaten without anything to back it up. It can be really frustrating."

"This happens a lot?"

"Well, yes. Like I said, it's about resources and budgets. You do what you can do with what you have. It's not just us. It's all of law enforcement, all over the country. Heck, probably all over the world. You have to make decisions about what to test, what evidence to collect. The realities are that those decisions often come down to what you can afford to process. I can't tell you how many rape test kits sit in evidence rooms, untested, for decades sometimes, because no obvious suspects have come to light in the investigation and the case isn't high profile or whatever. There just isn't enough money to test them all. Sad, but painfully true."

He stared at her incredulously. "That's terrible."

"I know, right? The sad thing is bad guys get off all the time because there's not enough money to throw everything you can at a case, forensically at least. But unless you've got bottomless pockets, I don't see how it can ever improve."

"Is that what was done in my wife's case? Evidence wasn't tested that should have been?"

Her hand froze with her tea glass halfway to her mouth. She slowly set it down and cleared her throat.

"We've gotten off track. That's not what I was specifically talking about."

"Really? So if this were your investigation to run, as you see fit, you wouldn't have performed additional testing?"

A light blush stained her cheeks. "It's not my investigation."

"But if it were?"

"Look, I'm still a newbie, okay? Six years on the force, but only two months as a detective. And I already told you, they haven't actually assigned me any of my own cases. I've done knock-and-talks and I type interview notes, things like that. But in the end, my opinion isn't worth much."

"It is to me. Don't you get it? Everyone else I've spoken to downtown is more concerned about placating me and getting me to leave, rather than share any meaningful information." On impulse, he took her hand in his. She jumped as if startled, but he didn't let go.

"What do you want from me?" Her voice was so low he struggled to make out the words.

"The truth, Willow. I've been living in limbo for years, living with lies. Please, tell me the truth."

Chapter Ten

The silence grew between Grayson and Willow as he held her hand like a lifeline. He felt as if he were on a precipice, ready to fall, and this smart, bold, amusingly sassy woman was the only one who could save him.

He leaned in closer. “Please, Willow. Help me.”

She let out a ragged breath as she tugged her hand free. “I don’t know if I can.”

He squeezed his fingers against his palm, surprised at the twinge of loss that had passed through him when she pulled away. “Try. That’s all I ask.”

She sat there a long time, uncharacteristically serious and quiet as she stared at the tabletop. Finally, she said, “I honestly don’t know if it will make a difference. I truly don’t. But the only potential way of generating more leads that I can think of is if you can get Chief Russo to send everything, every piece of physical evidence that was collected in your family’s murder, to a lab for testing.”

“I saw something about DNA testing in the binder. One of the reports said that the killer didn’t leave any DNA at the scene.”

"No DNA *that the police found.* That doesn't mean there wasn't any." She held up her hands as if to keep him from interrupting. "In most cases, it doesn't make sense to test everything. Like when you already have a suspect, other corroborating evidence. But in your case, with no leads and nothing to go on, throwing everything you have at it is the only option. I'd like to see more testing done just in case there's that one item with DNA on it that could break the case wide open."

"Wide open? Really?"

"Well, a crack is more realistic. Even if DNA gives you a suspect, you still have to build a case, find out if they had motive, opportunity. But it could at least give you a starting point."

"Which is more than I have now."

"Exactly."

"What evidence should be tested that wasn't already?" he asked.

"I remember reading that there were some bloody, smeared fingerprints on the inside of the front door that were deemed not useful, meaning not enough detail to upload to AFIS."

"AFIS?"

"Automated Fingerprint Identification System. It's a nationwide database courtesy of the FBI. If there were good prints, with enough identifiers to upload to AFIS, then anytime potentially matching prints are found, either now or in the future, an alert would be sent to Gatlinburg PD."

"What's that matter if the prints that were found aren't good enough to upload?"

"It doesn't. But if this were my case, I'd send the prints to the FBI to examine. They're the true experts in that field. Maybe they'd be able to identify more unique areas of the prints—whorls, arches, ridges, in specific sequences—that might make an upload possible."

"You don't sound very hopeful."

She shrugged. "It's admittedly a long shot. No guarantees."

"You must have brought it up for a reason. You were talking about DNA when you mentioned the fingerprints."

"Right. I was kind of thinking out loud. It would have been great if those prints could have been swabbed for DNA testing. But it dawned on me that wouldn't work. Swabbing for DNA destroys fingerprints. Dusting for fingerprints degrades DNA." She sighed. "I wish they'd chosen the DNA route in this instance. But since they didn't, at least taking the prints to the FBI for further analysis is one more thing to try. Of course, that's only if we had access to test the evidence, which we don't."

He leaned back against the booth. "Then it probably *is* hopeless."

"I didn't say that. But I don't want to give you false hope, like Jeffries gave you, thinking Katrina might still be alive." She blinked. "I'm so sorry. I shouldn't have said it that way. She could be alive. She really could be. I sincerely mean that. It's just, well, being honest here, the odds aren't good."

"Willow, have you found something or not?"

She grew quiet as if gathering her thoughts, or deciding whether or not to say anything else. When she finally looked up at him, she had a determined look on her face. "Here's what I'd do, if I could do what I wanted. I noticed on the evidence logs that your wife's clothes were saturated with blood. Knowing now that she was cut, not just shot, those clothes should be tested again, more extensively. They should take swabs from every part of them to look for the killer's DNA."

He slowly nodded, understanding the logic of what she was saying. "If the knife didn't have a substantial enough guard to stop his hand from sliding down the blade, it's highly *likely* he would have cut himself. The knives I carry on missions always have a guard for that very reason. My personal knife does too. I'm surprised the police didn't think about that."

"Your personal knife? You carry one with you?"

"Always."

"You didn't have one when I arrested you."

"Only because I'd just been at the police station. I didn't want to set off the metal detectors when I went inside. Normally, I do carry a knife."

"Okay, well, back to the DNA. The shirt was swabbed. But not extensively. It's a judgment call, a resource issue."

He shook his head in disgust. "Lack of resources is a poor excuse for not solving crimes."

"Agreed. But when you only have so much money to go around, you have to make tough choices. Do additional testing on a crime that seems solvable, or spend all your money on one that doesn't."

"Every case should get the same attention," he argued.

She held up her hands. "Just playing devil's advocate. I see these dilemmas every day at work. It's not fair to paint the police as the bad guys when they're doing the best they can with what they have."

"Then they need more resources."

"Yes. They do."

"What if I offer to pay for the testing?"

She shook her head. "That would open them up to lawsuits. Families who can't afford to supplement the police budget to help with their loved ones' cases would be disadvantaged. No police chief is going to touch that."

He swore. "So there's nothing I can do."

"That's not what I'm saying. If we can somehow steer Jeffries toward realizing a specific test might yield him a suspect, he might argue for the budget for it. Like touch DNA, for example."

He shook his head. "I feel like we're going in circles. What's touch DNA?"

"It just means a really small amount of DNA can now be detected where we couldn't before. Like when you touch a piece of clothing and the oils on your skin are left behind. Touch DNA technology on that spot of fabric might yield a profile good enough to put in CODIS—"

"You're losing me with all this terminology. What's CODIS? Another FBI database?"

"Combined DNA Index System, and yes it's maintained by the FBI. It pairs DNA profiles with information on known violent offenders. It's searchable, like AFIS. My point is that if the person isn't in CODIS, or local DNA databases that don't link up with CODIS—"

"Isn't all law enforcement hooked up to the FBI databases?"

"Not even close to all. Big cities, sure. But there are thousands of small-town sheriff's offices or police stations that have only a handful of employees and little crime. It doesn't make sense to go all high-tech in their situations. Which means you could have collected prints but not get a match in the major databases, even though that person's prints are on file at some rural sheriff's office two counties over. I've heard of cases solved by homicide cops sending their fingerprint cards to fifty or more other jurisdictions to have them manually checked against their own systems."

"I'm starting to wonder how any crimes are ever solved."

"It's not as easy as crime shows make it look, that's for sure. It's a lot of long hard hours. And you can only do what you have the budget to do."

"It all comes down to money again."

"And know-how. I'm not even sure TBI has the right people in their labs who can use the latest, greatest forensic techniques that science has to offer. The equipment alone is horrendously expensive. And the people have to be trained how to use it. The only reason I know about a lot of this stuff is because I'm a forensics nerd. I've studied all kinds of ways to solve crimes using the latest innovations. But most agencies, including Gatlinburg PD, can't afford to take advantage of them." She held her hands out in a helpless gesture. "I'm sorry, Grayson. I think we've hit a dead end."

He sat back, thinking about everything she'd said while she absently tapped at the ice cubes floating in her tea. She looked as defeated as he felt. It was unbelievably frustrating to think there might be some technology available to point to a suspect in his wife's and daughter's murders, but he was powerless to do anything about it, even though he had more money than he could possibly spend in ten lifetimes.

Wishing he'd ordered something stronger than tea, he turned to pick up his glass when a red newsbreak banner running along the bottom of one of the TVs caught his attention. It was an update on the River Road Rapist case. There'd been another attack late Friday night while he and Willow were reviewing his wife's murder book.

He caught Willow's attention and motioned to the broadcast. "I thought the police had the rapist in custody."

Her face drained of color. "No, no, no. That can't be. The guy confessed."

"One of those false confessions you mentioned earlier, maybe?"

She shoved her glass back, her expression a mixture of grief and anger. "I hate that someone else was hurt. Jeffries sounded so certain he had the right guy. Last I heard, they were waiting for his DNA results as confirmation. Maybe if they'd been able to get the tests done more quickly, they would have realized the real rapist was still on the streets. And they might have been able to do more to keep the public safe."

They sat silently as the waitress cleared their table, promising to return soon with the check.

"Grayson?"

"Hmm?"

"You mentioned earlier that you'd hired private investigators before but they came up empty-handed. Who did you hire?"

He laughed harshly. "Who did I not hire? I used six different companies. That's one of the reasons your chief and your boss are so sick of me. Each time I hire someone new, they start at the station, grill your boss with questions."

"Did any of them come up with anything at all that was useful?"

"No. Nothing. Not a single suspect has ever been identified, or even suggested."

"Maybe you need to hire different investigators."

"I wouldn't know where to begin. My track record isn't exactly stellar in that area."

"What about the Justice Seekers? They're a private company operating out of Gatlinburg. I'm not all that familiar with them but I know they do some types of investigations. Jeffries mentioned you might know the owner."

"Mason Ford. I sold him a parcel of land on Prescott Mountain to build his new home. I did speak to him once about working my wife's case. But he prefers to keep his team focused on helping the living, people who are victims themselves and in immediate danger. He provides bodyguard services and tries to figure out permanent solutions so they no longer have to live in fear—like a woman on the run from an abusive ex—cases where the law can't be proactive until after the crime occurs."

"He wouldn't make an exception to help you?"

He shrugged. "He probably would if he thought he could do any good. He doesn't feel that anyone on his team has the expertise to work something that cold with so little evidence to go on."

"That's a good point. I hadn't thought about it that way. You need someone with a proven track record working on cold cases. And, of course, you need access to all the collected evidence."

"What if I sue Gatlinburg PD for access?"

"I can't imagine you'd win. The police have every right not to turn over evidence. Testing can consume it, destroy it. If the defense team can't repeat the same tests, using their own experts, they can argue for the test results to be thrown out."

"What does it matter if we never even *get* to trial?"

She held up her hands. "I'm on your side. The problem is that you're a civilian. And civilians can't be responsible for evidence in an open investigation, cold or not." She frowned, idly tapping the table. "Civilian." Her expression turned guarded, but thoughtful. "I have an idea. It's pretty out there. I'm not even sure it's feasible. And it would cost a boatload of money."

"I'm not sure how much a boatload is, but money won't be a problem. What's your idea?"

She held up her fingers and ticked them off one by one as she spoke. "To solve a cold case, you need investigators experienced with cold cases. To have access to police evidence, you need someone active in law enforcement as a liaison. To get the evidence properly tested, using the latest techniques and eliminating the long wait times, you need a lab at your disposal." She grabbed his arm, excitement sparkling in her eyes. "Address those three things—cold-case experience, law enforcement access to evidence, private lab—and you've got everything in place to work your wife's case."

He stared at her. "Are you saying I should create my own company to solve cold cases, and partner with someone in law enforcement?"

"That's exactly what I'm suggesting. There'd have to be a contract between the company and the police. But if it's a partnership, with some kind of active law enforcement liaison who maintains the chain of custody on the evidence, it might work. And don't forget the lab. You'd probably need to fund your own, a private lab."

"Has that ever been done before? Do you think the police would go for that?"

"There are a handful of private cold-case companies in the country. But as far as I know, none of them have partnered with police the way I'm talking, where you'd get access to test all of the evidence and use your own lab."

"Why would they agree to it? You already said I

can't just throw money their way for preferential testing."

"You wouldn't be giving anyone preference over anyone else. You'd have to agree the company would work on cold cases, *plural*, not just yours. They'd all be given the same treatment. I'm thinking you can limit the geographical area to the Eastern Tennessee region. That's thirty-three counties, but most of them are small without significant population centers, so it wouldn't be nearly as overwhelming as it sounds. As I said, every case would get the same attention, the same access to testing. It's a way to solve the resource issues without opening the departments up to lawsuits. The police get a better case-clearance rate. You get the best of the best trying to solve your wife's murder. Win-win."

"Yeah, well. Even if they'd agree to something like that, I don't know the first thing about cold cases. We both know my lousy track record of hiring the wrong investigators. I'd have to hire a consultant to get this right, to make sure I set up the company, and the lab, in a way that the police will agree to do business with me. I wouldn't have a clue who to hire to help me do that."

"Too bad I'm not in the market for a job," she teased.

He stared at her, considering.

Her eyes widened. "Don't look at me like that. I wasn't angling for a job offer."

"Why not? I could double, triple your current salary."

She blinked. "You don't even know how much I make."

"I've seen your apartment. You don't make much."

"Ouch."

He smiled. "Doesn't matter. Name your price. Like you said, I'd have no clue how to get something like this off the ground without you. I mean, sure, I know how to establish a business, hire the right human resources people, accountants, that sort of thing. I've got a dozen companies in my portfolio right now. But setting up a cold-case unit? I'm at a loss. I need you, Willow. What will it take to get you to work for me?"

"Pay off my student loans for starters." She chuckled.

"Done."

Her smile faded. "I was joking."

"I wasn't. I'll pay off your loans, triple your salary, and throw in a six-figure signing bonus. With standard benefits, of course, including a 401(k)."

She stared at him, her mouth open.

"The sooner you say yes, the sooner we can start working on our plans."

She grabbed her drink, then frowned when she realized it was empty. She grabbed his, and gulped down the last of it.

He smiled. "You seem a bit overwhelmed."

She clutched the edge of the table for a moment, then turned in her seat to face him. "I am. It's an amazing offer, truly. Mind boggling, even. But the answer is no."

Surprised, he waited for more. When she didn't explain, he prodded, "Because why?"

"Because… I already told you. I'm not in this job for the money. I'm in it to help people."

"You can help people in the private sector just as much as in the public sector. What do you have against making money?"

"Nothing. I'd love to not have to worry about bills, to have an apartment I can turn around in without bumping into a wall. But I don't want to throw away what I've been working for my entire adult life. Do you have any idea how hard it was to make detective? The last time Gatlinburg PD hired a new detective was fifteen years ago. Making the team was my holy grail. But I'm not done yet. I still need to prove I can cut it with the big boys."

"You said yourself they're not letting you run with any cases. You're a detective in name only."

"Wow. Thanks for that."

"Sorry. I didn't mean you aren't qualified, or that you aren't trying. Obviously you've won me over talking about how you'd approach my wife's case. What I meant was that you're not being allowed the opportunity to help people and prove yourself the way you want to. I can help with that. I can give you free rein, to be what you want to be, no one standing in your way. And before you say no, again, think about this. You said you're a forensics nerd, that you've been wanting your department to pursue new technologies. From everything you've told me, that will likely never happen."

Her mouth tightened. "Probably not."

"But if you help me, if you're in charge of all the detectives—"

"In charge? You want me to be the boss over your investigators?"

"Of course. This cold-case company is your idea. Your baby. I'll run the business part of it, all the stuff necessary to establish a corporation and make sure we're in compliance with tax laws and regulations. You'll be in charge of hiring decisions, establishing the team, setting policy for how to approach each case, how to choose what cases to work, whatever makes sense for an investigative unit."

"What about the lab?"

He shrugged. "We'll figure it out together. I can build a brand new one—"

"That would take too long. It would be better if you can partner with an existing one. Maybe fund a new wing, new techs. Make an agreement that your cases take top priority but they can use the new wing to supplement other cases when it's not being used for our cases. I mean, your cases."

"*Our cases* sounds better. What do you say?"

She still seemed hesitant. "It sounds like a dream. If you're serious about paying off my student loans—"

"I am."

"And the six-figure signing bonus?"

"I'll wire the funds to your account as soon as you give me your banking information."

She swallowed, her hands fisting in her lap. "If I quit my job, I'm burning a bridge with Gatlinburg PD.

I'll never get a chance to be a detective again, not for them. Once your wife's case is solved—"

"I love the sound of that," he said wistfully.

She smiled. "I'd like nothing more for you. But I have to look out for myself, as well. After her killer is brought to justice, you have no incentive to keep the cold-case business going. It'll be hugely expensive, a drain on you financially. You could shut it down and I'd be unemployed with no prospects. It's not like I could go to another police department and start out as a detective. That's not how law enforcement works. You have to go through their academy, walk a beat, pay your dues and hope you eventually—years down the road—pass their detective's exam. After that, you still have to wait for a spot on the team to open up. Even then, you may get passed over and the position goes to someone else."

"Is that what's holding you back? Fear for the future?"

"That's a good way of putting it, yes. It's hard to turn down everything you've offered, especially because I'd get to mold a detective unit, establish it as cutting-edge, use the best technology science can offer. I'd be able to help far more people than I ever could in my current job. But if it's a temporary position, I have to say no."

"I see your point. And it's a valid one. I can't swear that I'll want to keep this new company going indefinitely. And it's not likely I could sell it to someone else who would. Few people can afford a cost center that doesn't produce revenue. Although I'd argue we could create a revenue stream eventually, by offering our services to civilians to solve their cases. But, regardless, I can offer you assurances, in writing. I can provide you with a golden parachute."

"A golden parachute? Like what CEOs get?"

"Exactly like what CEOs get. It's a clause I'd put in your contract that ensures if you were ever fired—which of course would never happen—or if I dissolve the company, you'd be compensated financially so you can land on your feet. I'd make sure you have a generous enough severance that you can start your own private investigation firm, if that's what you want to do." He smiled. "And we haven't even talked about the best part."

"The best part?"

"If you agree to work for me, you'll no longer be working for Jeffries."

Her lips parted in a delighted smile. "You're right. That *is* the best part." She laughed and threw her arms around him, hugging him tight.

He froze, shocked to feel her soft curves pressed against him.

As if sensing his hesitation, she pulled back, but only slightly, her gaze searching his. "It's just a hug, Grayson. Nothing to feel guilty about. It's okay to hug me back. We're just two friends, celebrating."

He stared down into her sparkling emerald eyes, surprised she could read him so easily, that she knew he felt guilty even thinking about holding her. And yet, that's exactly what he wanted to do. He needed, *craved* the feel of her in his arms. And until this moment, he'd never even realized it.

Her smile turned sad. She loosened her hold.

No. He wrapped his arms around her and hauled her against his chest. She made a happy sigh and snuggled against him, her arms tightening once again. He let out a shuddering breath and rested his cheek on the top of her head. For the briefest of moments, he pushed away the concerns and worries, his conscience telling him this was wrong. Because it didn't feel wrong. It felt… wonderful. He closed his eyes, reveling in her warmth, breathing in the clean scent of her hair. And he allowed himself the fantasy of believing that he mattered to someone again, if only as a friend.

She was the one to end the hug and scoot back in the booth. It stunned him how empty he felt after she let go. He had to clench his fists to keep from reaching for her.

What the hell was wrong with him?

She smiled. "See, that wasn't so bad, was it?"

He cleared his throat, twice, until he could trust his voice again. "Was that a yes, then? You'll take the job?"

She chuckled. "That was definitely a yes."

"Great. I'll have the contract ready in a couple of days." He forced a smile, uncertain what to do next. He knew what he *wanted* to do, pull her against him and hold her again. And that absolutely terrified him.

He desperately looked around for the waitress, but didn't see her. "She should have brought the check by now."

"I can go ask the hostess to find her."

"No need." He pitched an obscene amount of cash on the table, desperate to escape, to put his world back on its axis. "Let's go."

Chapter Eleven

Willow watched through her apartment's kitchen window as the black Audi sped out of the parking lot. Poor Grayson. She'd shaken him badly with that hug. When she'd pulled back, the look in his deep blue eyes had nearly broken her heart. He'd seemed so… lost, confused.

The conflict warring inside him was all too apparent in those stormy eyes. He'd wanted her—maybe sexually, maybe not. She wasn't sure. But he'd desperately wanted that human connection of holding and being held. Too bad he was drowning in guilt and couldn't free himself to live in the moment, to be happy.

She shook her head in wonder. What kind of love that must be, to not be able to move on after so many years. And what wouldn't she give to be loved like that one day? Her parents were probably the only couple she'd ever met who even came close to that kind of relationship. It melted her heart every time she saw them share a secret look across a roomful of people as if no one else were there. It had always made her smile and long for what they had.

But now, after seeing Grayson, and how much he was suffering, she wasn't so sure. She wouldn't want to be that miserable if the love of her life passed on before her. And she wouldn't want him unhappy, longing for her. She decided then and there that if she ever was lucky enough to fall in love and marry her soul mate, she'd customize her wedding vows. She'd make her groom promise not to pine for her. She'd make him swear that he'd try to find love again and not allow himself to feel guilty over it. After all, love was a gift, the kind that only flourished when it was shared.

"There you go, Willow," she chided herself. "Waxing poetic when you have a million things to do."

Like craft her resignation letter to turn in on Monday.

But first, there was something else she had to do, follow up on a hunch. It had been bothering her since noticing a faded picture on a bulletin board flyer at the restaurant. But she wasn't sure why. Now, little alarm bells were going off in her head as the puzzle pieces started clicking together. But she had to be sure.

She hurried into her bedroom for her laptop, then set it on the coffee table. As the ancient computer took its time booting up, she drummed her fingers impatiently. She really needed a new one. This one was barely limping along.

Once the screen finally flickered to life, it took another agonizing five minutes of searches to find a news website that actually had a picture of the woman who'd been attacked Friday night.

She was in her late twenties and small in stature. Her hair was long, brown and hung in waves halfway down her back. She appeared to have a mixture of Caucasian and possibly Korean ancestry. In the picture, she was well-dressed, the quality of her clothes clearly better than average. And the gold earrings she wore didn't look cheap by any stretch.

Willow pulled the piece of paper out of her pocket that she'd taken from the restaurant and smoothed it out on the coffee table. It was old, faded and wrinkled, but the picture was still good enough to make out the woman's features.

This couldn't be a coincidence.

She grabbed her phone and punched the speed dial for her boss.

He answered on the first ring. "What do you want, McCray?" He'd obviously recognized her number. "We're kind of busy here. There was another attack last night and the whole River Road Rapist team is here trying to figure out what we missed. 'Cause the guy who confessed obviously ain't the perp."

"I saw a news report about it. You've seen her picture, right?"

"I'm working the case. What do you think?" His tone dripped with sarcasm.

"Sorry, right. Of course, you have. Will you please bring up her picture on your monitor?"

"McCray—"

"Please. It's important."

He sighed heavily, but she could hear him tapping his computer keyboard. "Okay. It's up. Now what?"

"Split your screen and pull up another picture beside it. It's from an old missing person's case, the one where the single mother went missing."

"Erin Speck? From two or three years ago?"

"Four, actually. And, yes. That's the one."

"That's a cold case. I don't have time for that right now."

"It'll only take a minute."

"Like I have a minute to spare." He mumbled something about rookies, but once again he tapped away at the keyboard. "What's got you thinking about that old case anyway?" He tapped a few more keys.

"I was in a restaurant tonight and noticed one of the old Speck flyers when I was heading to the ladies room. I'd just seen a news report about the latest attack and—"

"Holy crap."

"You have it? Both pictures?"

"In living color. Holy. Crap."

She tightened her hands on her phone. "You see what I see, then? It's not my imagination, right?"

"No, McCray. It's not your imagination. Erin Speck and last night's rape victim could be twins."

"Erin was an only child, and she wasn't adopted. So they definitely aren't. I know Wagner had already theorized the rapist has a specific physical type he goes after—mid-twenties, pretty, nice clothes, nice jewelry. And they all have long dark hair. But we all thought the rapes started six months ago."

"I'm not a newbie, McCray. I can connect the dots. But I don't like where they're leading."

"I know, I know. We thought we had a serial rapist on our hands, who went too far with one victim and killed her. If Speck is dead, which seems likely, and her case is linked—"

"Then our serial rapist is also a serial murderer," he said. "And he's been operating in our area a lot longer than we realized. Dang it. We're already up to our elbows in this. Going back four years to work a cold case isn't going to make it any easier. We don't have the resources for that."

"I know. I'm sorry."

"Don't be. McCray, I know I'm hard on you, probably harder than I should have been. But this, this is good work. I'm glad you called and told me."

She blinked. "Um, thank you, sir. I appreciate that."

"Enjoy the rest of your weekend off. It may be the last one you have for a while. Come Monday morning, I'm putting you to work on this case along with the rest of us. The training wheels are coming off. We need you." *Click.*

Willow slowly lowered the phone. Training wheels? *We need you?*

Her hand shook as she shoved her hair back over her shoulders. Had she misjudged Jeffries this whole time? Had he been giving her gopher duties as part of her training, trying to ease her into becoming a full-fledged detective? All along, she'd thought he was being petty, punishing her because his boss had forced him to hire her when he'd wanted to hire his nephew instead. Could she have been wrong?

Monday morning, he planned to assign her to a case—*the* case—the most important one they had. She was finally about to become a detective in reality, not just name, something she'd despaired of ever doing while working for Jeffries.

And she'd just promised Grayson Prescott that she would work for him, and quit her job with Gatlinburg PD.

What had she done?

Chapter Twelve

Willow took a long look in the restroom mirror, trying to get excited about returning to the Gatlinburg PD conference room down the hall for the supposedly final round of negotiations. If everything went as planned, she and Grayson would leave today with all of the contracts signed. *Unfinished Business*—cop slang for a cold case, and the chosen name for Grayson's new company—would finally take off.

But even though Willow's fancy new business suit and hair styled into a single braid that fell halfway down her back made her look professional and polished, the butterflies in her stomach told the real story.

She was terrified.

Terrified that she wasn't good enough. That she'd given up her job three months ago for nothing. That she would let Grayson down, that a year from now, two years from now, he'd still be living in limbo with no one brought to justice for the murder of his family.

She braced her hands on the granite countertop. Three months. Had it really only been three months ago that she and Grayson had come up with this outlandish plan to start a cold-case company? After that night at the restaurant, she'd somewhat reluctantly resigned from her job as a detective, which Jeffries seemed to take as a personal affront, saying she was quitting at the worst possible time. But she couldn't turn her back on Grayson. Jeffries had a team to help him. Grayson had no one.

Looking back, it had been the right decision. The link between the River Road rapes and the Speck case, though seemingly strong, had yielded nothing new in their search for the rapist and killer. Gatlinburg PD was getting nowhere with their investigation. But in that same time, she and Grayson had made tremendous strides toward the start of something special that would help so many hurting families.

If they could just get the contracts signed.

The men and women here today were the proxies with the final say-so about making the partnership agreement for the entire East Tennessee region. But instead of signing the contracts in front of them, they'd spent the last hour listening to the lowest ranking person in the room—Sergeant Jeffries.

He really knew how to hold a grudge.

He obviously couldn't stand that the lowly detective he'd once berated was now rubbing elbows with millionaires, a governor—courtesy of an introduction by Mason Ford—and higher-ups in TBI who wouldn't even take Jeffries's calls. No doubt, part of that resentment was also because she'd earn more in a year working for Grayson than Jeffries would in a handful of years in the public sector. And as a result, as an invited guest of the Gatlinburg police chief, her former boss was doing everything he could to sabotage Grayson's chance at justice for his family.

The alarm went off on her watch, which she'd taken to wearing at Grayson's suggestion. She had to admit, it looked great with her suit. And it seemed more professional to subtly glance at her wrist instead of hauling out her phone when she wanted to check the time. Right now, the alarm was telling her the break was over. Everyone would be heading back to the conference room. Which meant she couldn't hide in here any longer.

She drew a deep steadying breath, then headed for the squad room to get to the conference room on the far side. But as soon as she stepped into the squad room, she stopped. The sight of Brian Nelson, the nephew of Sergeant Jeffries, sitting at the desk that used to be hers shouldn't have bothered her. After all, she'd known he was her logical replacement since he'd scored the second highest on the detective's exam—right below her. But knowing it, and seeing it, were two different things.

Brian said something to the detective at the next desk, then noticed her standing by the doorway. He smiled and waved as if they were old friends. She waved back, pretending—like him—that they didn't despise each other. They'd never been friends. Not even close.

There'd certainly been an attraction, on his part, several years ago. And he'd been relentless in his pursuit of her, asking her out so many times she'd lost count. But even though he checked off all the boxes on paper, in person there was something about him that made her stomach churn with dread. Admitting to him that she wasn't physically attracted to him had stopped the date requests. But it hadn't been a good strategy for forging a successful working relationship on the rare occasions that their paths actually crossed.

And when they'd both gone up for the detective slot, and she was the one hired, his resentment of her had only gotten worse. Now, seeing that he'd taken her old job, she couldn't help feeling bothered by it. And a little icky, knowing he was touching the chair, the desk, sticking his hands inside drawers that had once been hers. She shivered and rubbed her hands up and down her arms.

"Ready to get this done?" Grayson stepped beside her from the hallway. "I think just about everyone's back from break. Are you ready?"

"I think so. But I'm not looking forward to it. Things have gotten pretty intense in there."

"Negotiations often are. Don't worry. They'll cave soon and sign on the dotted line."

"I hope you're right."

"Trust me."

"I do." She squeezed his hand, something that would have made him pull away in panic weeks ago. But now he simply squeezed back. Baby steps. He was slowly rejoining the land of the living, smiling more, growing comfortable around her. She'd given him hope. And she prayed that hope wouldn't die today at the hands of Jeffries, or someone else in the meeting determined to end the promise of Unfinished Business before it even started.

Half an hour later, in response to yet more questions from Willow's nemesis—Sergeant Jeffries—Grayson was reviewing the proposal again for the twenty-odd people stuffed into the conference room.

He fanned out the files on all of the investigative professionals who'd tentatively agreed to sign on as part of their new company, assuming the cold-case unit became a reality. He tapped them one by one, discussing their merits, trying to get the meeting back on track.

"Ladies and gentlemen, you and your respective agencies have been consulted and kept up to date on everything Ms. McCray and I've been doing to create Unfinished Business. We've shared our preliminary plans for the headquarters facility that will be built on Prescott Mountain. We've received verbal agreements with all thirty-three counties in Eastern Tennessee to partner with the new company."

He raised another folder. "This is a contract with one of the best private labs in Tennessee. I'm funding the creation of a new wing of equipment and professionals to focus on testing for cases being worked by Unfinished Business. But I'm in no way taking away from their ability to help other agencies. Instead, I'm adding to their capabilities by allowing them to use that new wing to augment their other work when they aren't conducting tests for us. It's a win-win, for everyone. So why are we still debating this? What's the real issue here?"

Willow leaned back in her chair, watching all eyes turn toward Jeffries again. Sure enough, he crossed his arms over his chest and gave Grayson a doubtful look.

"All of us met earlier today without you, a pre-meeting," Jeffries announced. "We wanted to see where we stand on this endeavor, see if we're in agreement. We realized the majority of us have the same concern. Namely, the involvement of Ms. McCray."

Willow stiffened, shocked that he'd let his dislike of her jeopardize something this important, something that would help the people in his own county.

Grayson's jaw tightened, a subtle signal that he was angry. But he did his best to cover it. "What exactly is the concern about her?"

"We're not confident in her ability to oversee your team of detectives when she has all of two months of experience as a detective herself. We think this cold-case unit would be doomed to failure if it's led by her."

Willow squeezed her hands together under the table. Jeffries had just vocalized the same fears she'd had herself on many occasions. But she knew her limitations, and because of that had researched extensively to find the right people to hire—people with far more experience than her, people specifically skilled with cold cases and impressive solve rates. She'd purposely taken on more of an administrator role to compensate for her lack of experience as an investigator. But apparently that wasn't sufficient for her old boss.

While she remained silent and focused on keeping her composure, Grayson wasn't nearly as accommodating.

The chill in his blue eyes should have frozen Jeffries where he sat. "Ms. McCray has years of experience in law enforcement, not to mention a master's degree in criminology with a minor in psychology. Do you have a master's degree, Sergeant Jeffries?"

Jeffries's face flushed. "My qualifications aren't pertinent here."

"Aren't they? You hired her as a detective on your team and yet here you are, criticizing her. Are you saying you made a mistake, that your opinions are flawed, unreliable?"

"Now, look here, Prescott."

"No, Sergeant, you look here. I'm not about to let your petty jealousies over your former employee's success destroy our chance to help families in Eastern Tennessee obtain the justice and closure that has been denied them for years. Through no fault of the TBI or any of the agencies represented in this room, budget constraints and lack of resources have meant the cold-case load is growing, not shrinking. Unfinished Business is the solution, a way to clear those cases and get dangerous kidnappers and murderers off the streets."

Grayson tapped the folders again. "Which of these investigators do you take issue with? Which one of these hiring decisions that Ms. McCray made doesn't meet your high standards?"

When Jeffries didn't answer, Grayson gave him a look of contempt, then addressed the others in the room. "We're ready, right now, to move forward. Even without our headquarters built, we can work out of my home. I've got contractors there right now converting my library into the work area we'll need. The investigators will have the latest, most advanced computer equipment. The team is ready to be here within days of us signing these contracts and will start working cases shortly after that. All you have to do is sign on the dotted line. Or is there something else holding you back that we haven't discussed?"

Jacob Frost from the TBI cleared his throat, gaining everyone's attention. "Let's lower the temperature in here a few degrees, shall we?" He gave Grayson a respectful nod. "First, I'd like to express my condolences again on the great loss you've suffered. I can well imagine how your frustration with your family's case going unsolved so long has led you to come up with this cold-case company as a possible solution. And I think I speak for us all when I say we genuinely appreciate that you're willing to front the resources to help countless others in similar situations."

There was a round of head nods and murmured agreement from the men and women sitting at the table.

"I sense a *but* here," Grayson said dryly.

"You'd be correct," Frost continued. "Regardless of whatever resentments may exist between Jeffries and his former detective, I can assure you those resentments have had no impact on the issue regarding Ms. McCray's qualifications."

Frost nodded at Willow. "Ma'am, no disrespect intended. I think you've done an incredible job helping Mr. Prescott with this idea. But there's a gap that has to be addressed. He doesn't have either a law enforcement background or experience as an investigator. And even though your education and experience in law enforcement are a tremendous advantage, you *are* relatively inexperienced, especially with investigations. Cold cases are some of the most difficult to solve, even with the most experienced of detectives. And you're asking all of us here to believe that the two of you have the combined ability to hire the right team for this job. That's just not realistic. I don't think any of us feel comfortable with what's been presented."

Grayson shot Willow a questioning look. But all she could do was shrug. She didn't know what to say.

He speared Frost with his hard gaze. "Every investigator we propose to hire has years of experience, much of that specifically working cold cases. We plan to liaison with law enforcement via your chosen TBI representative who will be an integral part of the team," Grayson reminded him.

"Understood. And I appreciate that. But that TBI rep isn't an employee of your company, and he or she won't have the power to oversee how the investigative team is being run, or to countermand the decisions. His or her job will be to focus on the legalities of whichever cases you're actively working and to ensure chain of custody is maintained on evidence. Your lead investigator will coordinate which cases to focus on and assign priorities. That requires someone experienced enough to judge the merits of each cold case presented by the various counties and determine which ones are potentially solvable. The success or failure is directly tied to the lead's decisions."

He gave Willow an apologetic smile. "I'm sorry, Ms. McCray. But all of us, without exception, believe it's safer, less risky, to have someone far more experienced in law enforcement *and* investigations to act as that lead." He looked at Grayson. "We'd like someone other than Ms. McCray to take on that role."

Grayson's jaw clenched. "Is that all or do you have more demands?"

"Not demands. Concerns and a few minor requests. The first is that before going public with this partnership and signing the final contracts, we'd like your team to solve some cold cases to prove that everything's in place that needs to be. We'd sign temporary contracts so you'll have access to the evidence in the chosen cases, of course. And then we'll make a decision about our continued partnership based on the success, or failure, of those investigations. That will be the true proof that the lead we're recommending, and the infrastructure you've put in place are compatible."

"The lead you're recommending?" Grayson gritted out.

Frost seemed unfazed by Grayson's less than receptive tone. "When we all discussed this earlier, the one name that kept coming up, the only one we could all agree on, was Ryland Beck."

Grayson frowned and glanced at Willow. "Who's Ryland Beck?"

Her face heated. "His name never came up during my search for investigators. I've never heard of him."

"Which goes toward your lack of experience, Ms. McCray." Frost smiled, as if trying to take the sting out of his words, before turning back to Grayson. "Beck is probably the best investigator we've ever had at the TBI. He began his career in Knoxville and eventually transferred to TBI where he worked exclusively on cold cases, for years. He quit because he was frustrated at the lack of resources to do his job, which makes me think he'd likely jump at the chance to work for your company, where resources won't be an issue. Another advantage is that since he's not active in law enforcement right now, you won't be poaching him from other agencies as you're doing with many of the investigators you plan on hiring." He chuckled, not seeming particularly upset over their so-called poaching.

"Getting Beck on board as your lead will go a long way toward making us comfortable with this planned partnership. Unfortunately, we really must insist that Ms. McCray no longer be in your employ, going forward, to ensure that she's not in a position to influence the investigative decisions."

Grayson stiffened. "Wait a minute, Frost—"

"This isn't up for argument," Frost insisted, his expression hardening. "Those are our terms. Obviously, it's your company. It's your choice to go along, or not, with our recommendations. But if you don't, then you'll proceed without the support of law enforcement."

Grayson's eyes flashed with anger. "You know damn well we can't be successful without access to case evidence, access we'll only get if you sign those contracts."

Frost pushed back his chair and stood. "Then I

guess you have to weigh that with everything else. I look forward to hearing your decision."

Willow sat frozen as everyone filed out of the conference room, leaving her and Grayson alone. She remained in her chair six seats down from him, her face flaming with embarrassment over what had just transpired. He sat rigid in his chair, his hands fisted on top of the table, lost in thought as he stared at the far wall. Neither of them spoke. What was there to say?

Three months ago, Jeffries had told her to enjoy her weekend off, saying it would be her last for a while. His prediction had turned out to be right, though not in the way he'd expected. Instead of working on the serial killer/rapist case, she'd been working with Grayson to make the cold-case company a reality.

They'd both toiled day and night, with her sometimes sleeping in a guest room at his mansion so they could get up early to work out some issue or brainstorm late into the night. She'd extensively researched investigators, searching for the cream of the crop, the best of the best. She'd interviewed dozens over the phone, then flew around the country with Grayson for the second and third rounds of interviews, whittling down their list.

Next, it was time to research labs. That part had been easier, since she and Grayson had agreed to narrow the scope to those within a three-hour drive of Gatlinburg. That would make it easy to transport evidence to and from the labs, considering their headquarters would be built here in Gatlinburg. But it had still taken weeks of phone calls, meetings and tours to narrow it down to two potential labs. The final decision had been difficult. But they felt good about their choice. Contracts had been signed, and the next step, the hardest one, lay before them.

Getting the TBI and thirty-three counties of law enforcement agencies to agree to their terms.

But they'd done it.

They'd met with the governor and dozens of other politicians to smooth the way and win their support. Then they'd conducted meetings with dozens of police chiefs, sheriffs and Jacob Frost—the all-important head of the TBI. It had culminated in today's final meeting with the leaders representing the agencies of Eastern Tennessee. Everything had finally come together. The pieces of the puzzle all fit. Except one.

Her.

She wasn't sure how long the two of them sat there in silence. Thirty minutes? An hour? Longer? But when Grayson finally let out a deep sigh and turned in his chair to face her, she read his decision in his tortured gaze, the tension lines carved around his mouth.

"Say it," she whispered. "I need to hear you say it."

"Willow, you have to understand. I can't live like this anymore, always wondering, never having closure. You've worked so hard. I know that. And this is killing me. But we're so close. We may never get this chance again and—"

"Say it, Grayson."

He swallowed, hard, shaking his head with regret. "I'm sorry, Willow. You're fired."

Chapter Thirteen

Grayson had spent an exhausting two months setting up the new cold case company without Willow's help. Between welcoming each member of the team, helping them find housing and pushing the contractors to finish converting the library into a squad room, he'd had little time for anything else. But now, finally, he had time to focus on what was most important, Willow.

He pulled his Audi into the parking lot and cut the engine but didn't get out right away. Instead, he allowed himself the guilty pleasure of watching Willow through the windshield.

She was sitting at a picnic table perfectly positioned beneath an oak tree where the sun wouldn't glare on her computer screen. Judging by the dark marks scored in the grass, she'd dragged the picnic table to that spot. He couldn't help smiling as he pictured her huffing and puffing, struggling to move something that outweighed her twice over. But that's the kind of person she was: driven, focused, determined to never give up until she'd reached her goal.

Kind of like him.

Except that *unlike* him, she hadn't betrayed the trust of someone she cared about in order to get what she wanted.

He sighed heavily and put his shades on before getting out.

He knew the exact moment when she realized he was there. Her hands froze on the keyboard. Her mouth flattened in a hard straight line.

"Hello, Willow. It's been a while."

She slowly looked up. "Two months isn't nearly long enough."

"I've been to your apartment a dozen times during those two months, but you never answer the door."

"Maybe I haven't been home."

"Your car was parked out front."

"I was probably washing my hair."

He chuckled. "What about all the phone calls? You never answer. Not even my texts."

"Maybe you dialed the wrong number."

He gave her a grudging smile. "Maybe I did."

She crossed her arms. "How did you find me anyway?"

"I bribed your neighbor down the hall. He said he's seen you in this park before and suggested I give it a try."

"Next time I'm keeping the pizza when they knock on my door," she grumbled.

"What?"

"Never mind. Now that you've found me, what do you want?"

"To talk. You look great, by the way. But then you always did."

Her eyes widened. "What are you doing? Sucking up to me? Let me guess. There's a report you need or minutes to a meeting that you can't find. It's all in that massive library of yours. Do the work. Hunt it down. Don't expect me to dig through drawers and cabinets for you. Or are you afraid you'll get your Armani suit dirty?"

"You do realize I spent years in the army right? In fatigues and combat boots. Hunkered down in rain and mud and burning hot sand, dodging bullets and taking out bad guys. Not a Louis Vuitton or Armani suit to be had. I'm not the snob you seem to think I am."

She rolled her eyes and bent over her keyboard.

He stepped closer to see what was on the screen. "Erin Speck? You're working on her case? On your own?"

"Not that it's any of your business, but yes."

"Why?"

She gave him an exasperated look. "Because I'm a detective. That's what detectives do. They investigate. Except I'm working for myself these days. Thanks to you convincing me to give up the job I'd worked for all my life, then, oh, yeah, firing me."

"Ouch."

She snapped her laptop closed. "Don't you have a headquarters building to design? Or lab equipment orders to place? Oh, wait, it's almost lunchtime. Maybe you and your buddy Frost have reservations, lobster for two at Nob Hill." She made a shooing motion with her hands. "Don't let me stop you. I wouldn't want you to be late."

"The whole bullets-and-fatigues speech didn't make a dent, did it?"

"Nope."

He sighed heavily. "You're not going to make this easy on me, are you?"

"Make what easy? I didn't invite you here. I don't *want* you here."

"I'm sure you don't. Lucky for me, it's a public park." He settled onto the bench across from her.

Her eyes narrowed. "You like this picnic table so much, take it." She tapped her computer. "By the way, thanks for the new laptop. I bought it with my golden parachute." She grabbed her satchel and flipped it open.

As she was reaching for her computer to stuff it inside, he put a hand on hers to stop her. "Willow, wait. Please. We need to talk."

She shook off his hand. "The last time we talked, you said *trust me*. Then you fired me. I'm not interested in anything else you have to say. We have nothing to discuss."

"I want to hire you back."

She paused with her laptop half inside the satchel and slowly raised her gaze to his. "Excuse me?"

"Firing you was reactionary, stupid and wrong. I've regretted it ever since." He looked at her over the top of his shades. "I'm not good at groveling. What will it take to get you to come back?"

"Don't insult me by offering more money."

"I wouldn't dare."

She folded her arms on top of her satchel, pinning him with her stare. "Having been burned, I've no intention of ever putting my hopes and dreams in your tender care again."

He winced.

"But," she continued, "I have to point out that you have a lot to learn in the art of groveling. You haven't even said you're sorry."

"I am, you know, sorry. More sorry than you can imagine."

"*Pfft*. Right. Let me guess. Something went wrong and you think I'm the only one who can fix it?"

"Actually, no. Everything's going like clockwork. Ryland Beck agreed to lead the team. Half the investigators are at my house. They're working in the converted library with the IT guys, setting up our computer system for tracking cases. The rest will be here in another week. Rather than having to wait for the lab's new wing to be built, I rented another building down the street from the current lab. Equipment's being set up. Techs are being hired. The team has already started on some initial so-called *easy* cold cases that Beck chose, to prove to Frost that Unfinished Business is worth partnering with. Plus, they're working one that's a lot more difficult, the same one you're working on—the Speck disappearance. With the potential tie-in to the active River Road Rapist case, he feels it would be a huge boon to the company to solve it."

Her eyes widened. "Congratulations. You definitely

don't need me. Jeffries was right." She shoved the computer in the satchel and zipped it closed.

"No. He wasn't. He was wrong, Willow. They all were—me included. I never should have given in to their demands. Without you, I'd still be floundering, with no direction, no hope. You're the reason Unfinished Business exists. And it's not right that you're not a part of it now. I'm sorry for what I did to you. I hope someday you'll be able to forgive me."

She stood and settled the satchel's strap across her shoulder and hip. "Your groveling's improving. You get points for that. Not that it makes a difference." She started to move past him.

He grasped her arm and waited until she looked up. "I don't want points, Willow. I want you."

Her eyes widened. "You…you what?"

He framed her face with his hands. "I didn't fight for you when I should have. But I came to my senses a few days later. I had a private meeting with Frost and convinced him to change the terms of our arrangement. As long as we have Ryland Beck on board, and we prove ourselves with the initial cold cases, he and the others will sign the formal contracts making things permanent. I want you back, Willow. Back at Unfinished Business."

She dropped her gaze to his chest and let out a shaky breath. "Wow. Okay. I'm confused." She pushed his hands down and stepped back. "About a lot of things," she mumbled.

"Like what?"

She opened her mouth to say something, then seemed to think better of it and cleared her throat.

"Willow? What questions do you have?"

"Um, mainly, how did you get Frost and the others to agree that you could hire me back? Assuming I'm even interested, which of course I'm not." She crossed her arms over her chest.

"I threatened him."

"You what?"

"I told him if he didn't back down from his stance about you, I'd go to the press and give them an exclusive on how a multi-million-dollar privately funded cold-case unit had been turned down by TBI, and that the escalating numbers of unsolved murders and missing persons cases in Eastern Tennessee would continue to rise out of control."

"You did *not*."

"I totally did. I even showed him a planned press release. He flipped immediately."

"Would you have done it, if he hadn't flipped? Would you have gone to the press?"

"In a second. Come back to work with me. You can be Beck's boss if you want, or choose another role. I don't care, as long as you're there. We'll be a better team with you on it. And if it takes groveling every day to make you happy and earn your forgiveness, that's what I'll do."

She raked a hand through her long dark hair, tossing it back over her shoulder. "You don't even need me."

"That's where you're wrong. Can Unfinished Business be a success without you? Maybe. Probably. But I know it can be better with you there, with your ideas, your creativity. And it's eating me alive that your creation is coming to life without you there to steer and guide it, and enjoy it."

She cocked her head, hands on her hips. "So, what you're saying is you want me to work for you so you don't feel guilty anymore. It's all about you."

He grinned. "That's one way to look at it, I suppose. What do you say? Will you do it?"

"Maybe. Let me sleep on it."

"I can live with *maybe*. Thanks, Willow. You won't regret it. Promise."

At her skeptical look, he winced again. "I know a promise from me doesn't hold a lot of water. But let me prove it to you. You really can count on me going forward. I won't let my desperation to solve my family's case influence how I treat people again. I've learned my lesson."

She blew out a long breath. "Okay, okay. I'll do it. But I get a ten percent raise."

"I thought more money would be an insult?"

"I changed my mind."

He laughed. "Deal."

He kept in step with her as she headed to her car.

"Speaking of your family's case..." She put her satchel in her back seat. "How is the investigation going?" She shut the back door and turned around, brows raised in question.

He focused on keeping his tone upbeat when he replied. "We aren't working on that case yet. Ryland was worried that it might not be solvable." He shrugged, trying not to let her see how crushed he'd been to hear the veteran investigator tell him that. "Since we need some quick solves under our belt to get the contracts signed, he chose cases he felt had a lot more promise. I can see his reasoning. We'll get to it, eventually. So, when will you be back at work? Can I look for you tomorrow morning?"

"Sounds good." She smiled. "And Grayson?"

"Hmm?"

"Thanks. The timing really sucked, but you finally stood up for me. I appreciate it."

Unable to resist the impulse, he leaned down and pressed a kiss against her cheek. "See you tomorrow."

WILLOW HELD HER smile until Grayson's Audi disappeared around a corner. Then she closed her eyes, holding on to her car door for support. Just seeing him again had sent her heart racing. She'd been ready to forgive and forget the second he'd stopped by the picnic table. Which, of course, only made her angry at herself, so she'd disguised her eagerness by forcing him to work for whatever it was he wanted.

And then he'd said he wanted *her*.

She'd been so stunned she couldn't put a coherent thought together. Thankfully, before she could throw herself in his arms, he'd clarified that he wanted her as his employee.

What was that for her now? Strike three? Four? Had she ever even been in the game?

She should have been immune to her ridiculous attraction to him that had morphed into a near-obsession

during their three months of working together. Him firing her should have been the cure. Instead, she'd pined for him. She was living proof of that absence-and-the-heart-growing-fonder thing. While talking to him beside her car, she'd just managed to get her emotions under control when he'd decimated her again with one tiny soft kiss. On the cheek.

If he ever really kissed her, it would probably kill her.

Not that there was any chance of a real kiss. He was always a gentleman, refusing to give in to the desires and longing she'd seen in his gaze. There was no room in his heart for her, only for a ghost.

She wiped her eyes, dismayed to realize tears were spilling down her cheeks. Crying over a man had never been her thing. But this man, Grayson Prescott, was worth a few tears. Not because he could slay her with a smile or make her shake with desire after a stupid hug or a friendly peck on the cheek. He was so much more than that. Smart, strong, caring, able to admit when he'd made a mistake. Well, eventually anyway.

And he didn't deserve to suffer the way he had, the way he was still suffering. It was so unfair that just when he thought he was going to get the dream team working on his cold case, Ryland Beck had steered them toward something else. Once again, Grayson had to wait for justice for himself, for his loved ones. She kind of hated Ryland right now and she'd never even met him.

She started up her car, which took three tries. Maybe

she should spend some of that golden-parachute money to replace her old Taurus instead of just her computer.

When she reached her apartment, she sat in her usual spot in front of the coffee table. Then she closed out of her investigation file labeled Erin Speck: Missing, Presumed Dead and opened the other file she'd been working on for the past two months—Maura and Katrina Prescott: Murder on Prescott Mountain.

Chapter Fourteen

Willow sat in the elevated glass-walled conference room in Grayson's converted library, looking from Grayson to Ryland as they filled her in on what she'd missed. Downstairs, a small team of investigators was working at their desks, a few of whom she'd interviewed months ago. Others, she'd never heard of until today.

"I don't understand. I thought we were going to have thirty-three investigators—one to work cold cases in each of the counties that we'll support."

Ryland shook his head. "That's too many. I know it seems counterintuitive, but less is more. With investigations, you need a manageable-sized team that can become close, a tight unit, complement each other's weaknesses and magnify each other's strengths."

He slid a folder across the table to her. "I know you introduced yourself to everyone in the squad room before coming up here, and seemed surprised that you hadn't met some of them during the interviews."

"Some of them? Try most of them."

He glanced uncertainly at Grayson before continuing. "Right. So the first page in that folder is a list of the final team members. All of their résumés are in the folder too."

She read through the list of names, then flipped the page over to see the rest. The back was blank. "Ten investigators? That's it?"

"That's the core team, the permanent positions. That includes you, of course, but not Grayson since he isn't an investigator. I'm also counting our TBI liaison to help with investigations since the liaison workload will fluctuate, depending on the needs of each case."

"I don't… I'm… confused. It seems like everything that Grayson and I worked so hard to plan has been tossed or completely changed."

Grayson leaned across the table and gently squeezed her hand as if to reassure her. "The basic infrastructure you and I came up with is still there. Just smaller."

"Exactly," Ryland said. "You did a great job, honestly. And I would have picked most of the investigators you wanted to hire if I wanted a team that large."

"*Most* of them? Meaning you don't approve of some of my hiring decisions?"

"No, no. Any of the ones you picked would have been fine. I just preferred some others, investigators I'd met over the years and with whom I was familiar."

She held up the piece of paper he'd handed her. "Those *others* are over half this list."

Ryland gave Grayson a help-me look.

Willow held up her hands to stop whatever he was about to say. "Don't. I get it. You both did what you felt was best in the months when I was gone. I'm just struggling to absorb all of this. Ryland, can you explain what you meant about a core team of *permanent* positions? That implies there will be others who come and go?"

"Exactly. The team will grow or shrink as needed, outside the core group. With each case we work, we'll bring in temporary experts if or when we need them. Like, say, a car accident scene reconstructionist. Useful for some cases, but probably not for most of the ones we'll work."

She slowly nodded. "Okay. That makes sense." Kind of. She decided not to argue about it since she didn't want to seem completely negative on her first day back. She held up the list again. "I see the TBI liaison is Rowan Knight. I remember meeting him. He seems like a great fit."

"I agree," Ryland said. "Once a year, TBI will rotate that position with a new special agent, just as you proposed."

Yay for her. He'd kept *one* idea she'd had.

Grayson motioned to another folder on the table. "I've hired administrative staff as well, assistants, a human resources manager, that sort of thing. They all start next week and will work out of another part of my home until our headquarters is built. We wanted the computer system and construction work completed before they got here."

"Sounds like a great plan." Had she made a mistake coming back? Had her feelings for Grayson clouded her judgment? They didn't seem to need her and she wasn't sure how she was going to fit in. It was obvious Grayson and Ryland had thought of everything with their plan to grow and shrink the team based on workload. She eyed the list of team members again, and the roles each of them filled.

"Anything else I can explain?" Ryland asked.

She glanced up. "Actually, I wanted to ask you about the Erin Speck case. I did quite a bit of work on that on my own and Grayson asked me to share it with you. I gave a flash drive to Faith, um—"

"Lancaster." Ryland smiled encouragingly. "Don't worry. You'll learn everyone's names in no time at all."

"Lovely." She gritted her teeth. It was the closest to a smile that she could manage.

He cleared his throat, clearly uncomfortable.

Grayson chose that moment to grin, which had her wanting to kick him beneath the table. She knew she was being childish. But was it really too much to ask that this Ryland guy could have at least one major flaw?

"Regarding the Speck case," she said, trying hard to keep the little green monster at bay. It wasn't Ryland's fault that he was offered the job she'd wanted for herself. But that didn't mean she had to warm up to him right away. "Grayson told me you only just started working on it a few days ago. But I wonder whether you've thought about what kinds of forensic tests you plan to run on the evidence collected from her car? That was the last place anyone saw her so I feel it's important not to overlook even the smallest item."

"Couldn't agree more. The first thing I did in her case was check on her car. The police returned it to her parents after processing. But her father was so distraught he parked it in the garage and wouldn't allow anyone near it."

His eyes lit with excitement. "It's basically a four-year-old *pristine* potential crime scene. That never happens. One of the forensic techs we hired at the lab went over every inch of the car, inside and out, and gathered prints that were missed by Gatlinburg PD. They swabbed every surface for potential touch DNA testing. One small fiber on the back seat appears consistent with a fiber found on one of the River Road Rapist's victims, which of course strengthens your theory that the cases are connected."

"I'm so relieved," she said dryly.

He shot her an uncertain look, obviously not sure whether she was being serious or sarcastic. At this point, she wasn't sure either.

"Right," he said. "Um, so we're also exploring a relatively new technology that might get some usable prints from the heavily patterned car seats. The computer software cancels out the repetitive sequence of the patterns to reveal latents. We're testing dirt and minerals from the tires and undercarriage to compare against soil-sample databases of the area. That might tell us where she'd driven the car most recently. If we can match that to any areas the rape victims traveled, it can help us expand our geographical profile as to where the perpetrator might live. Aside from that, of course, we're reinterviewing everyone who knew her, reconstructing the timeline of the weeks before she disappeared, looking at financial and cell-phone records, triangulating places to search based on last cell-phone tower pings. You know, all the standard stuff."

Her inner mean girl wanted so badly to criticize him for something. But he was doing everything she'd have done, and then some. "Sounds like you're on top of things, Ryland. I appreciate the update and am sure I'll have more questions later. But I need to talk to Grayson in private for a moment, if that's okay."

"Of course. I've got plenty to keep me busy. Let me know if you need anything."

If she smiled any harder, her face would probably break.

When the door closed and Ryland jogged down the stairs to the main floor, Grayson burst out laughing.

She crossed her arms. "I fail to see what's funny."

"*You*, sweet Willow. If looks could kill, Ryland would be a lump of burning coal right now."

His unexpected endearment had her belly fluttering. But what he'd said about Ryland had her cringing with embarrassment. "Was I that obvious?"

"He couldn't get out of here fast enough."

She groaned. "Dang it. He'll hate me now."

"He'll love you. How could he not?" He winked. "What did you want to talk to me about? Or was that an excuse to save Ryland's life?"

She had to force herself to breathe after the how-could-he-not-love-her comment and the devastating wink. One day soon, she'd have to tell him to stop smiling so much and not to wink, hold her hand or—God forbid—hug her. Otherwise, her heart would never survive. Would he ever be able to let go of his past and see what was right in front of him? See *her*?

"Willow?"

"Sorry. Still trying to take everything in." She tapped the member list. "I noticed no one's taken the victim's advocate position. Seems like an essential role to me. I wouldn't want the family of a victim to hear that a cold-case company is working their case by hearing about it in a press conference."

He leaned back in his chair. "You're right. We haven't hired one yet. I didn't see the urgency since we're keeping the company a secret until the final contracts are signed. You disagree?"

"No. That makes sense. And I'm kind of glad you haven't filled the position yet. I'm having a hard time seeing how I'll fit into the team. Maybe the advocate slot would be good for me, and Ryland could hire another investigator to replace me in that role. I've got a minor in psychology. That should come in handy."

"I think you'd be a great victim's advocate. But I thought you wanted to be more hands-on with the detective work."

"I did. I do, eventually. But I'm also a realist. You've got some of the best investigators in the business on this team and I'm still a novice. I can contribute more in the advocate role than as an investigator. At least until I—"

Her phone chimed. "Sorry. I'm expecting an important text so I kept the sound on. Just a sec."

"No problem."

She checked the screen and her stomach dropped as if she'd just leaped off a cliff.

Grayson leaned forward, his brow furrowed with concern. "What is it? Did something bad happen?"

"That depends on your perspective."

"Business or personal?"

"Business."

"I'll get Ryland—"

"*No.*" She winced. "Sorry. That came out louder than I meant it to. It's just, I think you should hear this first. Without him."

"Okay. What's going on?"

She tapped the table, trying to figure out the easiest way to explain it. "Have you ever heard of the Golden State Killer?"

"I'd be living in a cave if I hadn't. He's been all over the news for the past few years. He raped and murdered people in California, in the '70s and '80s, I think."

"That's right. Then he disappeared off the radar. No one ever even had a suspect in the case and decades passed. Then a cold-case unit took a fresh look. They already had a DNA profile of the perpetrator from evidence collected at the scenes. But it never generated any hits in those FBI databases I told you about."

"But they caught him using DNA, didn't they?" he asked. "If I remember it right."

"They did."

"You're not suggesting he's the guy we're looking for are you? He's been in prison a while."

"No, I'm not. The only reason I brought him up is

because of how he was caught. I think it could be the key to catching our guy too. It's called forensic genealogy. It's where you take a known DNA sample, like from a rape kit, and you upload the DNA profile to one of those popular ancestry family tree database websites."

"I've used those myself," he said. "Helping my niece trace our roots. She's convinced if we look hard enough, one day we'll find she's royalty."

She smiled. "How old is this little princess?"

"A very precocious six." He motioned for her to continue. "Didn't mean to sidetrack you."

"I just wanted to point out that if someone in the extended family of our serial rapist happened to have uploaded their DNA profile to one of these websites, and we upload the DNA profile of the rapist, we can get a familial match. We know these two people are related somehow, so to figure out who the rapist is, we work on the family tree of the known familial match to try to eventually trace to the suspect. That's how they caught the Golden State Killer."

She held her hands out to the sides. "I'm hugely oversimplifying the process. It takes a ton of work to build the tree and find those links between the two DNA samples. It's based on a combination of math, probabilities and genetics as well as old-fashioned detective work, interviewing people, performing surveillance to get more information on various family members. You build an online genetic profile and extrapolate from there. It's grueling work. If I tried it on my own, it would probably take me a year, if I'm lucky.

And once you narrow it down you could potentially end up with a large number of people who could be your perpetrator. Then you weed them out by figuring out who lived where and when, who had opportunity, things like that. If you get a workable number of potential suspects, then you try to get their DNA samples to see if there's a match."

He nodded. "I remember they followed the Golden State guy until he spit on the sidewalk to get his sample."

"You're probably thinking about another case where they did that. But his was similar. They swabbed the door handle of his car while he was shopping in a Hobby Lobby. And later they tested a tissue from his trash, to confirm their findings. Both samples matched their rapist's DNA profile, so they were able to get a warrant to get an official DNA sample they could use in court. The rest, as they say, is history. He's never getting out of prison."

"I take it you want to try this family-tree stuff on the rapist case."

"I do. I know it's not technically a cold case, but since it appears that our cold case—the Erin Speck case—may have been done by the same guy, it makes sense to use the DNA profile from the rapist case and move forward to save time. And once Ryland gets test results from Speck's car, if he's able to get a DNA profile, that will hopefully match the one we already have. Solve one case and you solve both of them. And hopefully get the perpetrator to tell us what he did with Erin."

"Sounds like a solid approach to me. We'll need to hire one of those experts—"

"A forensic genealogist."

He nodded. "I can't imagine Ryland having an issue with that."

"Actually, he won't need to hire one. I already did. During the past few months when I was working the Speck case by myself, I used part of that ridiculously generous golden parachute money you gave me to hire the best person I could find."

"Why didn't you say that to start with?"

"I wanted you to understand the context before I explain this next part." She leaned toward him, her excitement warring with dread. "Grayson, that's what the text I just got was about, an update from the genealogist. A while back, she found a familial match on an ancestry site and she's been building the family tree ever since to come up with a pool of possible suspects. She just texted me that she's narrowed our potential DNA contributor to six males on the family tree."

His eyes widened in surprise. "You've got a list of suspects, and there are only six?"

She nodded.

"Good grief, Willow. That's fantastic. Why didn't you want to tell Ryland?"

"There's a…complication."

He waited.

"Keep in mind, with this ancestry thing, the genetics only get you so far. The bulk of the work after you get your starting and ending points is to build a family tree, which is based on siblings, marriages, births, all of that. The tree starts with science, but after that it becomes an exercise in drawing a map, essentially showing different branches of the tree that the genes would have gone down. Are you following?"

"I'm trying."

"Think of any typical family tree. It's like an umbrella. Your great-great grandfather and great-great grandmother are at the very top. But as you follow it down, you have to trace their siblings, then their children, and their children, all the way down each rib of the umbrella. You could end up with hundreds of people on that one little tree. All you know for sure is that each of those tips on the bottom has a very distant relationship to the great-greats at the top."

"Now I'm following. I think. You're saying this genetic expert knows our killer is one of those points at the very bottom, because they're related to someone who uploaded their DNA to this database at the very top of the tree."

"Pretty much. Our genealogist works through that math I was telling you about in order to eliminate some of the branches of the tree. And she can eliminate some others because of obvious things—like a certain branch ended with all females. Or another one ended when all of the males in that line died before the timeline for our crime."

"I'm with you," he said. "She figured out the suspect has to be at the end of a handful of specific branches, but she can't narrow it down any further. Our investigators will have to do that."

"Exactly. We have six people, all male, who fit an

age range where they could be capable of committing these rapes and murders. Because of marriages all along the tree, they don't all share the same last name either. We're talking distant cousins who may not even know each other. Investigators need to look at each of the six to try to rule them in or out. Of course, getting a DNA sample from each one would be ideal so they can zero in on a specific suspect more quickly."

"All of this sounds like that magic clue we've wanted all along to make the pieces of the puzzle fall into place," he said. "So why do you seem so worried?"

"Not worried, exactly. More like…concerned…at how this is going to play out. It could actually hurt our company's reputation before we've even begun because they'll question the research."

"They?"

"You'll understand when you see this." She opened the text app on her phone. "Here's the suspect list we need to research." She slid the phone across the table.

He looked at the screen and swore.

"My thoughts exactly."

He shoved his chair back and stood. "We need to talk to Chief Russo. Right now. I'll call him on our way downtown so he can clear his calendar."

She hurried after him. "Should I grab Ryland, tell him to come with us?"

"No. Your instincts on this were spot on. The fewer people who know about it for now, the better. At least until Russo decides how he wants to proceed."

Chapter Fifteen

Police Chief Russo sat behind his desk, staring at the text on Willow's phone for a full minute as if the names would change if he looked at them long enough. Finally, he handed it back to her without saying anything.

Grayson glanced at Willow to judge her reaction. She flashed him a worried look, obviously unsure what to do next.

Grayson cleared his throat. "Chief Russo—"

Russo held up his hand to stop him. "Don't worry. I'm not going to shoot the messenger." He glanced at Willow. "Or in this case, messengers, plural. And you don't need to go into another drawn-out explanation about the science behind forensic genealogy. When that Golden State Killer case made the news, the first thing I did was study up on how they figured out who he was. Seemed like a clever way to catch someone. I just never thought it would be used to catch one of my own guys, or his *son*." He shook his head. "What a mess."

He stared down at his desk. "If one of my men *is*

the perp, it's going to shake the foundation of trust between the police and this community. It could take years to rebuild." He swore. "I don't get it. It doesn't even make sense. If it's a cop—or even the cop's family—you'd think he'd know to be careful, not to leave behind trace evidence that could point back to him—especially DNA."

"These days," Willow said, "it's exceptionally difficult not to leave any trace evidence behind. The amount of DNA required to yield a viable profile is minuscule. A drop of sweat, a hair with the follicle attached, saliva. He *did* try to be careful. He used condoms, covered his features until he got his victims blindfolded so they couldn't identify him. But it's almost impossible to attack someone so violently, to lose control and get in a frenzy the way his victims have described, and not leave something of himself behind. His Achilles' heel, the thing that will bring him down, is that he thinks he's being careful and covering his tracks when he really isn't."

He shook his head in disgust. "This animal, regardless of who he is or who he works for, needs to be locked up before someone else is hurt or killed. Grayson, you said we can use your lab for the testing. And they can get the results back in hours instead of the days or weeks we're used to? Heck, months sometimes."

"Absolutely. Since we know three of the suspects are in Gatlinburg, I've already got a tech on the way here. Once the samples are collected, he'll head back to the lab. It's a couple of hours away, so the drive time will delay us. But we may still be able to get results on these first three by nightfall."

"And the other three? You don't have addresses for them?"

"Not yet. As soon as Willow gave me the list, we called you and headed here. I still need to brief my team about what's going on and get them working on locating the others."

"We can help with that."

"Thank you, sir."

"I don't like waiting, Grayson. We've got DNA collection kits here. One of our guys can collect the samples and an officer can hightail it down the highway, lights and sirens, to intercept your lab tech. Your guy can take custody of the samples and head back to his lab and start the testing. You okay with that?"

"Better than okay. Are you sure you can convince your men to provide a sample without a warrant?"

He made a derisive sound. "They don't have a choice if they want to keep their jobs. That's part of the agreement when they sign on here, that if they're ever a suspect in a crime they'll fully cooperate with the investigation and submit to any required tests. If they refuse, I can fire them immediately. And I don't even need a union rep to do it. The hard part will be the son, since he's not an employee here. But I don't see him wanting to jeopardize his father's job. He'll agree to provide the sample."

He punched a button on his desk phone. "Molly, have one of our crime scene guys come up here with two DNA swab kits. And tell Sergeant Mike Jeffries and his nephew, Detective Brian Nelson to come to my office, ASAP."

Twenty minutes later, a visibly shaken Sergeant Jeffries watched as the tech who'd swabbed his mouth for a DNA sample sealed it in the test kit and signed it.

"Where's your nephew?" Russo demanded. "He should have been here by now."

"He's not at his desk and didn't answer my text yet. Maybe he's interviewing a witness out in the field and has the sound off on his phone." Jeffries cast a worried glance at Willow and Grayson. "But you don't need to test him. Not if you're going by that ancestry tree thing Mr. Prescott talked about."

"Explain," Russo said, his tone brooking no disobedience.

"Brian's not my sister's biological child. He's adopted."

Russo sat back in surprise. "Well. That's something I didn't know. Mr. Prescott, I'm no expert but that does seem to rule him out. No blood link. No DNA link. No need to test. Do you agree?"

Grayson glanced at Willow. "Are you okay with that?"

"I can't think of a reason to argue otherwise. Looks like Brian is in the clear."

"Excellent," Russo said. "One name off your list." He gave Sergeant Jeffries a hard stare. "Your DNA should clear you from that list."

"Yes, sir. It will."

"It had damn well better. What about your son? Steve? How fast can you get him here for his test?"

Jeffries swallowed. "Should be here soon, sir. When I texted, he said he had to find his boss to let him know he was leaving. His job is ten minutes from here."

"When he arrives, send him downstairs to our techs. They'll swab him there. I want to know the second it's done so I can have a uniform drive both of your samples to Mr. Prescott's lab."

"Yes, sir." He headed to the door.

"Jeffries?" Russo called out, stopping him. "Kick your team into gear and catch this guy so I can get the mayor off my back, will you?"

Jeffries gave him a nervous smile, nodded at Grayson and Willow, then hurried out the door.

Russo tapped his desk. "Even though I don't like you finger pointing at anyone in the department, I must say, Grayson, I'm already impressed with your new company. You figured out this rapist has been operating for years instead of months as we'd originally thought. And you've provided suspects when we had none. When we get this guy, we'll get some flak from the media for not getting him sooner, considering how quickly your company was able to solve this thing. But I don't even care. What matters is getting this monster off the streets. I look forward to seeing what you do next."

"Thank you, sir. The praise goes to Ms. McCray. Not only was the company her initial idea, she's the one who linked Erin Speck's disappearance and the

River Road Rapist. And the forensic genealogy part was all her too."

Willow aimed a grateful smile at him.

Russo stood and leaned over his desk, holding his hand out to her. She looked surprised, but she got up and shook his hand.

"Thank you, *Detective*. I say that title out of respect, regardless of who you work for. You've earned it."

She blinked, her eyes suspiciously watery. "I really appreciate that, sir."

"No one here ever doubted you'd do great things. I know Mike—Jeffries—can be a pill to work for. But behind closed doors, he bragged on you all the time. It's our loss that you decided to go into the private sector. But we'll reap the benefits as you help solve our cold cases."

She glanced at Grayson again, clearly rattled.

Grayson shook Russo's hand. "As soon as the lab calls us with the DNA results, I'll have them call you too."

"See that you do."

In the car on the way back, Willow sat uncharacteristically silent, staring out at the rising little puffs of white mist that gave the Smoky Mountains their name.

"You're shocked that Sergeant Jeffries bragged on you to the chief, aren't you?" he asked.

"I don't think shocked quite covers it." She looked away from the window. "What surprises me even more is that Brian's not our guy. As soon as I saw his name on the suspect list, everything clicked. I was sure it was him. He always put off a strange vibe, gave me the creeps."

"You don't think it's Jeffries? Or his son?"

"No on Jeffries. He can be a jerk, but he's a cop to the core. As to his son, I didn't even know he had one until today. We didn't exactly sit and swap family stories when I worked for him."

He chuckled. "I imagine not. Jeffries doesn't strike me as the bad-guy type either. And I've never met Steve or Brian. But I trust your instincts. We'll keep Brian in mind for future cases."

She laughed. "Sounds like a good idea. Honestly, it's a really good thing that we have DNA so we can tell the good guys from the bad guys. We've become so civilized that we've lost the ability to rely on our instincts about people. We open our doors because someone's dressed nice or has a friendly smile, never suspecting the evil that can lurk just beneath the surface."

Grayson tightened his grip on the steering wheel.

Willow's hand was suddenly on his shoulder. "I'm so sorry. I swear I wasn't thinking about what happened to your wife and daughter when I said that."

"It's okay. And it's not like I haven't wondered about the same thing. I've never been able to make sense out of why she opened the door. She had to trust whoever was on the other side, especially since the blood evidence shows she must have been holding Katrina at the time. She had to know her killer. But I've spoken to everyone I can think of, let alone whoever the police spoke to. No one has ever come up as a suspect. It just doesn't make sense."

She settled back in her seat, turning to face him as much as her seat belt would allow. "Before we got the suspect list and went downtown, there was something I wanted to talk to you about. When we get to the house, after we brief Ryland on what happened, can you squeeze me in on your calendar for a private meeting?"

He steered around a curve in the mountain before glancing at her. "You sound worried. Is it about Unfinished Business? Your role on the team?"

"No, nothing like that. It's something I've been looking into for the past few months that—"

Her phone chimed. She silenced it without looking at the screen. "I've been working on another case and—" Her phone chimed again. She swore.

Grayson chuckled. "Maybe you'd better check it. Someone's determined to get in touch with you."

"Sorry. I'll make it fast."

Grayson maneuvered the Audi around another treacherous curve as Willow's fingers flew across her screen, texting back and forth with someone. He doubted it was about the case. They couldn't have DNA results back yet. As far as he knew, they were still waiting for Steve Jeffries to show up at the police station for the cheek swab.

Her warm fingers were suddenly branding him through his shirtsleeve. "Grayson?"

The despair in her tone had him glancing sharply

her way. She'd gone pale, her green eyes luminous with unshed tears. "What is it, Willow? What's wrong?"

"We're too late."

"What do you mean? Who was on the phone?"

"Chief Russo." She drew a shuddering breath. "Another woman's been abducted. It looks like it's the River Road Rapist."

Chapter Sixteen

"The missing woman's name is Nicole Paletta," Grayson announced to the Unfinished Business team in the converted library of his home, after introducing Willow more formally than earlier, and explaining what had happened at the police station. Willow stood beside him on the steps to the conference room, so they could both see everyone as they briefed them.

"Paletta matches the same general description as the other victims of the River Road Rapist," he continued. "She's young, in her mid-twenties, well-dressed, upper middle-class and has long dark hair. She's single, no children, which is consistent with some of the previous victims, although some, like Erin Speck, did have children. What makes this particular victim so important is that we have a witness to her abduction, and we know it's one of five possible suspects."

He held up his hands to stop the flood of questions that he could sense was coming. "Willow can brief you on the pertinent details and answer questions. I just want to make clear, first, what our role will be in terms of helping bring Ms. Paletta home safely."

Willow gave him an encouraging nod as he continued.

"I know you all signed up to work cold cases. And you're doing a great job working to clear some so-called *easy* ones already. Plus, you've made great inroads on the Speck case. But we've all learned, thanks to Willow's observant eye, that our cold case—the Speck investigation—is related to the active case, the hunt for the serial rapist and murderer. I feel it's far more important to help the police find Ms. Paletta than to focus on our cold case. I hope you're all in agreement with that."

Ryland stood at his desk and looked around at the others before responding. "We're all ready and willing to do whatever you need us to do."

"Thank you. I appreciate it. The police are in charge of the search for Paletta. They'll coordinate with search-and-rescue teams, the TBI, and they'll have every law enforcement officer who's available out looking for her. They're the lead on the case, as they should be. Our role is different. We're going to use every resource at our disposal to suggest places for the police to search, based on our in-depth knowledge of each suspect."

"What in-depth knowledge?" Ryland leaned back against his desk, ankles crossed. "None of us have even been told about any suspects. Plus, if there's an eyewitness, can't they pinpoint which of these suspects you mentioned abducted the victim?"

"That question's my signal to let someone actually experienced in investigations and police procedures take it from here. Willow?"

He stepped back and leaned against the railing while she brought the team up to speed on the work she'd done with the genealogist. Her explanation was much shorter and to the point than when she'd explained it to him. Likely that was because everyone else in the room already knew about the science behind forensic genealogy.

"Regarding the witness," she said, "I think it's a waste of our time to pursue that angle. Maybe the police can get a better description or more details from her. But what I was told was far too generic to be helpful. Paletta was jogging down a street just off River Road when the witness saw someone yank her around the corner of a building. As is typical of this serial rapist and murderer, the man who accosted her was dressed all in black with his face covered. The witness didn't know whether the suspect forced her into a car or into one of the buildings. She just disappeared. That's it. The only reason we even know we have a victim, and know it this fast, is because the witness was her friend and saw the attack. They were jogging together, but the friend had fallen behind. She wasn't close enough to help but she immediately called 911."

Ryland motioned to let her know he had a question. "How can we be sure that the man who abducted Paletta is the serial rapist? If we make that assumption, and we're wrong, couldn't we be heading down the wrong path and wasting our time?"

Willow gave him a pained look. "Believe me, that's my worry too. One of the hallmarks of what we're doing here, working cold cases, is that we should have the luxury of taking the time we need to look under every rock, sift through all the evidence, explore every possible scenario. We don't have that luxury with the Paletta abduction. This man has killed before and could kill again. Time is not on our side. We have to make that uncomfortable best guess and do what we can to help. Grayson spoke to Chief Russo a few minutes ago on the phone. Russo specifically requested that we focus on the list of rapist suspects, so that's what we're going to do. Now, for that suspect list."

She held her phone out toward Ryland. He hurried forward and she pitched it to him.

"That text shows their names," she said. "Ryland, it's your team. How do you want to proceed?"

His fingers seemed to fly across her phone screen. Then he jogged up the steps and handed it to her before turning to face everyone else. "Guys and gals, I just texted that list to our message group. You should all have it on your phones now."

Willow chuckled. "Guess I need to get in on this message group for future reference."

He smiled. "Quick question. There are six names on the list, but you said there are only five suspects?"

"Brian Nelson can be eliminated. We found out he's adopted, so his DNA wouldn't be a match."

"Got it. Okay, this is what we're going to do, folks. We'll split into five teams with each team focused on one suspect. Use that fancy computer system Grayson bought for us that links up dozens of law-enforcement and private databases. Tap into social-media accounts, online newspapers, ancestry records on the public family-tree sites—all the usual places."

Willow touched his shoulder, interrupting him. "I can have the forensic genealogist send the team the tree information on these suspects. That should save some time in coming up with family members to contact."

"Thanks," Ryland said. "That'll definitely help. Nobody worry about making reports or presentations perfect or pretty. This isn't about documenting evidence for a prosecution. It's about saving a life. I don't care if your final research notes are chicken scratches on a napkin, as long as you can interpret them for the rest of us."

Ryland glanced at a large digital clock on the back wall. "It's a quarter till. Let's huddle up in exactly one hour and info-dump what we have. I want to know everywhere these guys have gone in the past month, from sunup to sundown and everything in between. Give me real-estate holdings, favorite fishing spots, where they each go on vacation. If they've got a lover on the side, I want to know where they go to fool around and all of the lovers' hidey-holes."

There was some good-natured snickering around the room.

Ryland grinned. "You know what I mean, ladies and gentlemen. Hiding places, love nests. That's the name of the game. We want a list of locations to give the police to search for Paletta, and we need it fast. Questions?"

Adam Trent, or Trent as he was known to everyone, stood to ask a question. "If we can narrow down the geography, that could cull the list of places to something more manageable for the police. We don't want to mention a cabin in Montana if the perpetrator wouldn't have the time or means to get there. Willow, can you tell us how soon after the abduction the police got moving on this? Did they lock down the highways, alert bus stations, airports?"

"Great question," she said. "Russo believes we caught a real break on this one. Within minutes of the abduction, highway patrol was stopping traffic and setting up checkpoints on all the roads in and out of Gatlinburg in a fifteen-mile radius around the city. They locked everything up tight and fast. He's confident our perpetrator is still in the area. Rangers in the Great Smoky Mountains National Park are patrolling campsites and hiking trails in case our guy tries to hoof it on foot. Police are going door-to-door downtown and in the foothills, checking every hotel room, business and doing their best to check private residences too. Any homeowner who isn't cooperative and won't allow a search is noted so police can keep a watchful eye for signs of our suspect in that location, or potentially return with a warrant if they have probable cause. The media has also been alerted, so that will put additional pressure on the bad guy to hunker down somewhere. Any other questions?" she asked.

Trent shook his head. "I'm anxious to dig in. I think we all are."

"You're speaking my language, Trent." Ryland threw a number out to each investigator, lightning fast, assigning them to five different teams. "Look at your suspect list. Team one takes the first suspect. Team two, the second and so on. Remember to ignore the Nelson fellow. Let's roll."

He hopped down the stairs and jogged to his desk. Soon the room was buzzing with conversations and the sound of tapping keyboards as each team huddled around a computer monitor.

Grayson shook his head in wonder as he stepped beside Willow again. "I wish the employees at my other companies were this enthusiastic about their work. No telling what we could accomplish."

She smiled, but it didn't quite reach her eyes. "Are you comfortable leaving them in Ryland's hands? I'd like to steal you for a bit."

"Investigating is growing on me, but it's not my wheelhouse. They're in good hands with Ryland." He arched a brow. "Is this about what you said in the car, before Russo's call? That you wanted to talk to me about something once we got to the house?"

She nodded. "Although wanting and needing are two entirely different things. Can we take this outside? Maybe scarf down one of your cook's amazing sandwiches by that English-garden maze while we talk? I always loved his creations when you and I were working here alone those first few months."

He gave her a sad smile. "I'm sorry about everything that happened."

"Don't be. We're past that now. I'm back, and I'm not going anywhere. To the garden then?"

His eyes took on a teasing light. "You always spent more time in that garden than I ever do. Maybe

I should ask my head gardener if there's something going on between you two."

She rolled her eyes. "I'm not Mr. Baines's type. I don't have leaves or branches."

He chuckled. "I'll grab the brown bags and some bottled water and meet you out there."

Chapter Seventeen

Grayson strode toward where Willow and his head gardener were sitting at the opening to the main garden maze.

"Thanks so much, Mr. Baines." Willow leaned across the little table that separated their patio chairs and squeezed his hand. "But be warned. If your advice can get my mom's violets to actually bloom again, she'll probably hop on the next plane and whisk you back to Lexington to solve all her gardening problems."

He chuckled and slowly climbed to his feet, knees popping like Bubble Wrap. "Better get back to work. The boss can be a real tyrant." He ambled toward one of the paths in the maze.

Grayson stopped beside Willow's chair. "You know I heard that, right, Mr. Baines?"

The gardener's laughter floated back to them.

"He seems like a really nice guy," Willow said. "Did he teach you a lot when you were growing up here?"

He set the bagged lunches and water bottles on the

table between them and took the seat that Baines had vacated. "He taught me plenty. With a willow switch on my backside."

Her eyes grew big and round. "He spanked his employer's child? With a switch?"

"More times than I can count. And I deserved every single swat. I was a terror, trampling his flower beds, nearly setting the woods on fire while lighting bonfires or trying to roast s'mores."

"Wow. Where were your parents?"

"Good question. I didn't see them a whole lot growing up. They traveled extensively, usually out of the country. And before you go feeling sorry for me, I had way more fun without them than I did when they were here. Baines was the perfect substitute father. He even built me an old fort way out in the woods, with real doors and windows. Pretty impressive. My mother would have been scandalized to know that I spent many a night there in a sleeping bag on the dirty floor with nothing to eat but the fish I caught in one of the ponds—courtesy of Baines and some of the other staff who taught me to fish and cook it too."

She blinked. "You can cook?"

He grinned. "I'm pretty good at it."

"But...you have a cook, a chef."

"Who worked for my parents even before I was born. If I have to pretend I can't feed myself so he feels useful, it's a small price to pay to salvage his pride. Besides, it wouldn't be fair to make him leave. This is his home." As she stared at him, his face grew warm. And it wasn't from the sun. "Stop looking at me like

I'm being noble or something. Anyone would do the same. It's the right thing to do."

She suddenly stood and crossed to him. Before he knew it, his arms were full of soft, curvy Willow, pressed against his chest, hugging him. He couldn't have pushed her away even if he knew it would cost his entire fortune to keep holding her. He didn't *want* to push her away. As he held her tight, he could almost feel the wall around his heart cracking open.

What was she doing to him?

When she stepped back, she shook her head in wonder. "You're a really good man, Grayson Prescott. Far better than most people know."

He cleared his throat. "Maybe we should eat before the sandwiches grow cold. Or warm. Or whatever. Heck, I don't even know what he packed for us."

She laughed and they both devoured their food, which ended up being hot ham and cheese on rye with some kind of fancy French sauce that elevated it to cuisine.

When they finished, the easy conversation was over and her expression took on an all-business look as she grabbed a folder from under the table.

"Ready?" she asked, her hands on top of the folder.

"That sounds ominous."

"It's just… It's some research I wanted to discuss with you."

He shifted his chair to face the table better instead of the shrubbery maze. "You do know about my lack of investigative skills, right? Harvard business school grads aren't the best equipped to solve murder mysteries."

"Harvard? Wow. No wonder you're such a snob." She winked to let him know she was teasing. After flipping open the folder, she pulled out a stack of pictures.

"Those look familiar."

"They should. This first one is Erin Speck. These others are the known victims of the River Road Rapist, including the woman who was killed."

Dread settled in his gut. "Known victims? You're implying there are more?"

"I am." She lined up the five known ones in a single row, side by side.

"It's amazing how similar they all look," he said. "Definitely a victim preference there."

"Part of his MO, his modus operandi."

She formed another row beneath the first, all new pictures he'd never seen before. And yet, they seemed achingly familiar. Young, female, with long brown or black hair.

"All these women were raped?" The idea was appalling, horrifying. And when she nodded, the sandwich he'd eaten seemed to sour in his stomach. "Any killed?"

"One." She tapped the middle picture. "Peggy Lidow. This other one—" she pointed to the picture to the left of Peggy "—is Samantha Stuckey. She's officially a missing person. Disappeared two years ago near Knoxville. All of them were either abducted, raped or killed in neighboring counties. They never came up on Gatlinburg PD's radar, or ours, until I went on a hunt to see if there were more victims we didn't know about."

"Why did you do that? Try to find more?"

"The gap between Speck's disappearance and the recent rapes was too long. The time between the rapes has been escalating. He's devolving, becoming more and more unstable. It didn't make sense to me that he'd abduct one woman, go three and a half years without attacking any others, then escalate so much in the past six months."

"Okay," he said, considering. "Using my fledgling detective skills, which are based solely on what I've seen on television, I have to ask what proof you have that these are connected? With Speck, the physical similarity to another victim was so strong it was creepy. And I know some fibers later proved it's the same guy. But what about these? You said they're from other counties. Is there DNA or something like that to link them?"

"The DNA from the one who was killed was too degraded to yield a useful profile. Rape kits were collected from the other victims but never sent to a lab for testing."

He fisted a hand on the table. "Resource and budget constraints again."

"Even you can't afford to fund every police agency out there. Resources will always be a problem in law enforcement no matter what we try to do to help. But in these specific cases, the similarities of their attacks, the fact that each was blindfolded, how their attackers subdued them, it all seems the same to me."

"Are you asking me to sanction testing their DNA, as part of the cases we're already looking into?"

"I am."

"You had to know my answer would be an emphatic yes. I completely trust you to use the company's funds in any way that you see fit. So what's the real reason I'm here?"

She reached for the folder again. As she flipped through it, alarm bells started going off inside him. When she pulled out yet another picture, he eyed it warily as she slid it facedown beneath the second row she'd created.

"The Speck case isn't the only one I worked on during my...break. I'd read a coroner's report about another potential victim of our serial rapist and murderer. And even though everything about the victim fit with the case we're working, one thing didn't. Her hair. At the time of her death, it was short, and blond." She searched his gaze. "But that wasn't always the case. When I was in your office one day, months ago, I noticed a picture on your desk. It was a picture of Maura. Something about it bothered me but I wasn't sure what, until I was researching your family's case on my own and thought about that picture. I searched the internet and found a copy of that same picture. You must have shared it with a reporter, because it was in a story he did about your family."

She slowly turned the picture over.

He stared down at the picture of his wife, the one

he saw every time he visited the mausoleum. The one her father had taken the day of their wedding. It shook him to his core as he scanned the two rows of victims above her. Every one of them could have been sisters.

And he'd never even considered a link, until now.

"She thought of herself as a rebel," he said, half smiling as he always did whenever she'd reminded him of that fact. "Her family emigrated here from Japan when she was a little girl. Like my parents, hers were strict, old-fashioned. They forbade her to dye or cut her hair. Or get a tattoo. So, of course, she did all of that. But out of respect for them, she'd waited until after we were married. Being rebellious at that point wasn't the big thrill she'd thought it would be. And she didn't like the work involved in constantly dying her roots. So for the most part, she kept her hair its natural color, black. And she'd grow it out. Until she got bored and cut it and bleached it blond again."

He forced himself to look up from her photo. "Mid-twenties, well-off, nice clothes, expensive jewelry. Long dark hair most of the time. But not when she was killed."

She gave him a sympathetic smile. "There's another difference too. Her hair, her blond hair, was violently hacked by the killer. There were tufts of it all over the foyer. It's one of the things that didn't fit, something that puzzled me. So I called a friend of mine, someone I met in my psychology classes. She's a consultant now, works with law enforcement. In her opinion, it's entirely possible that whoever killed your wife saw her first with long dark hair and fixated on her."

"Then what?" he asked. "He decided to kill her because she dyed her hair blond?"

"What's more likely is that he chose her as his next victim, possibly even his first victim ever, when her hair was dark. He didn't know she'd dyed it. When he knocked on the door, he expected the woman he'd fantasized about. Instead, a woman with short blond hair answered. It incensed him, destroyed his fantasy. He went into a frenzy, chopping her hair. She's the only victim who was shot, but she was also stabbed, which is consistent with the other attacks. I could be wrong—"

"But you could be right."

"If I am, then we need to have her clothes tested, like we've wanted all along. We need to do everything possible to try to find some DNA the killer left behind. The good news is that if we can get the profile, and it matches the one from the River Road Rapist cases, we already know the killer's identity. Or, we will, once your lab tests the swabs and provides the profiles."

"The suspects from your list."

"Exactly."

He sat back and stretched his legs out in front of him. "I should be relieved that we might be close to solving her case. But I kind of want to break something right now. It's revolting and infuriating that my wife, and my little girl, could have been killed because some sick animal liked, or didn't like, her hair."

He pushed to his feet. "Thank you. This is incredible, everything you've found. But I have to say, I don't know how you do it, day in and day out, dealing with this ugliness. I saw horrible things in combat, awful things. But this, somehow this is worse. Maybe because it's women, and in one case, a child. I don't know. If I investigated this stuff all the time, I'd be a complete basket case. Hell, I *am* a complete basket case. I need a minute."

He didn't wait for her reply. He strode back to the house and didn't stop until he'd reached his office. He stared for a long time at the picture on his desk, the same one that Willow had shown him in the gardens. He feathered his hands over it, then grabbed a round crystal paperweight sitting beside it. He clenched his hand around it, over and over, as hard as he could, trying to calm the rage inside him.

Such a senseless, useless waste of life. Over *nothing.*

He crossed to stand a few feet from one of the floor-to-ceiling windows, trying hard to cage the beast that Willow's words had set free. It was a beast he was familiar with, the rage and cruelty he could unleash on an enemy on the battlefield and never blink an eye. It was the pent-up frustration and resentments from his childhood that hadn't been nearly as idyllic as he'd allowed Willow to believe.

He'd had a love-hate relationship with his parents, mostly hate where his father was concerned. And he'd dreaded every time they returned from one of their trips. When they left again, he'd hide away in his room until the bruises faded. Once they had, he'd try to forget he even had parents. He'd play in the woods, spend his nights in the fort, exchange ghost stories with the staff.

But the rage was always there.

It was why he'd joined the military, hoping he could channel that anger into something constructive. The medals gathering dust in some closet upstairs proved that he had. But now he wanted nothing more than to let go, to let it fly, to scream to the heavens about how unfair it was that all those people—especially Maura and Katrina—had suffered and died at the hands of a crazed killer, over something as random and petty as whether he liked, or didn't like, their hair.

A knock sounded and the door opened behind him.

"I'm so sorry to bother you," Willow called out. "But I thought you'd want to know this right away. Some of the DNA test results are already back. Grayson, we've got a match."

He slowly turned to face her, his fingers tightening around the paperweight. "Is it Jeffries?"

She hesitated. "Yes."

He stared at her, the rage building. "Your old boss, a cop, raped and killed those women? Maybe even my wife? My child?"

"No, Grayson. He didn't. His *son* did."

He let out a guttural roar and hurled the paperweight through the window.

Chapter Eighteen

Willow sat beside Grayson in Chief Russo's office, waiting for him to arrive. She slid another sideways glance at Grayson before looking away.

He let out a deep sigh. "I'm not going to break another window."

"I didn't think that you were."

He speared her with his stormy blue gaze. "Are you afraid of me now?"

She stared at him, sensing the pain and worry beneath the thin veneer of civility he was struggling to maintain ever since she'd waved the red flag of his wife's murderer's name in front of him.

Desperate to break through the wall he'd erected around himself since learning about Jeffries's son, she did something she'd wanted to do since the first moment she'd realized he really was trying to save her in that back alley. She did something crazy, completely inappropriate given the current situation. And the only thing she could think of to try to reach the sweet, gentle man drowning beneath all that anger and pain.

She kissed him.

Really kissed him.

She leaned across the arms of their chairs and plastered her breasts against his chest. She poured all the love she'd been trying to deny into that kiss, letting him know without words that he *was* loved, that he mattered, that she trusted him. Completely. Unconditionally. No matter what.

And that he could trust himself.

He wasn't the animal he thought himself to be after losing control in his office. The self-loathing and shame that had crossed his face after he'd shattered the window had been quickly hidden behind a wall he'd thrown up between them ever since. She knew he was hurting, that he was embarrassed. And she wanted him to know he didn't need to feel guilty about anything.

He made a strangled sound deep in his throat, and then he was kissing her back. He was wild, almost savage in his response. But he didn't hurt her. Never that. His hands speared through her long hair, pulling her head back, giving him better access. Then he thrust his tongue inside, stroking her into a frenzy as his hands slid down, down, down.

She jerked against him, his expert touch setting off a fire inside her, sizzling across her nerve endings. Good grief, if they didn't stop she was going to tear off his clothes and straddle him right there in the police chief's office. With an unlocked door. And half the police force in the squad room just outside.

She broke the kiss, her chest heaving as she stared wide-eyed at him from six inches away, her hands clutching the arms of his chair to keep from falling. "Ho...ly...cow."

His lips curved in a slow sexy smile. "I'm guessing this means you're not afraid of me."

She snorted, then gasped in dismay at the ugly sound.

He grinned. "You're utterly adorable. If you were trying to distract me, mission accomplished." His smile faded as he gently smoothed her hair back. Then he cupped her face and kissed her again. A soft achingly sweet kiss that had her wanting to weep from the beauty of it.

When he pulled back, he ran his thumb across her lower lip in a caress that was almost as devastating as his wild kiss. She shivered in response, then lightly bit his thumb.

He drew a sharp breath, his body taut as a bow against her. "When this is over, we really, *really* need to talk."

"Or...something." She winked.

He laughed, then sobered at the sound of approaching footsteps.

She plopped down in her chair, hastily smoothing her shirt and hair. Grayson simply tugged his suit jacket and shoved a hand through his hair. Once. It fell expertly into place. No one would look at him and suspect he'd been practically devouring her thirty seconds ago. And here she was, still frantically finger-combing her hair.

When the door opened, she quickly dropped her hands. Russo marched in, followed by one of the court reporters Willow had met a few times before. Sergeant Jeffries slinked in behind them. He shut the door, no doubt not wanting his peers to hear the upcoming conversation. Not that they wouldn't find out eventually.

Grayson watched Jeffries's every move like a predator ready to attack. Willow placed her hand on his forearm, not caring one bit if Russo or her former boss noticed or what they thought of it. She wanted Grayson to know she was there for him, no matter what.

Russo plopped into his chair and ordered Jeffries to sit in a chair on the left side of the room, beside the court reporter who set up her steno machine on the edge of the desk.

Willow and Grayson were sitting on the right side. Luckily for Jeffries, it was out of slugging range. Because no matter what Jeffries planned on saying, neither she nor Grayson believed he couldn't have known about his son and what he was doing to those poor women.

Russo introduced everyone for the court reporter's benefit. After explaining that an official record was being made of the meeting, he motioned to Willow.

"Tell us what the lab told you. To save time, I already told our court reporter, on the record, about the whole genealogy thing you explained earlier today. You can add to that and then I'm going to fill in some blanks you don't even know about."

She glanced in confusion at Grayson, then turned to the chief. "I'll keep it as brief as I can. The genealogy work indicates that one of the six suspects we've come up with is the rapist and killer we're all looking for. This morning, DNA swabs were taken from two of those people—Sergeant Mike Jeffries and his son, Steve Jeffries. I received a call from the lab this afternoon stating the test results were back on those samples. Both were negative. They didn't match the killer's profile. However, Sergeant Jeffries's profile revealed a close familial link to the killer's profile, a father–son link. So the lab concluded there *is* a match, to Steve, pending a retest. His original sample must have been contaminated somehow and he'll need to provide a new sample. In the meantime, it would be prudent to arrest him now—if you haven't already—to ensure he doesn't go on the run."

Russo crossed his arms on top of his desk. "And I agreed with that suggestion when you explained that on the phone earlier. So I've got Steve downstairs on a twenty-four hour hold. But there's a problem. You see, while waiting for your lab to perform the testing earlier today, our guys did some digging on Mike and Steve, alibi checking, pending those DNA results. At the time of three of the attacks, Steve has a rock-solid alibi. He was out of the country for work."

Grayson straightened. "Then you need to check his alibi again. Something's not right."

"I agree with you. Something's definitely not right. So I had my guys recheck the alibi. There is no mistake. Mike's son, Steve, couldn't have raped or killed those women." He speared Sergeant Jeffries with a frosty look. "Which is why I sat down with Mike, here, and asked him to explain what the hell was going on.

DNA doesn't lie. Turns out, Mike's a liar. Steve isn't his only biological son. His *other* son is Brian Nelson."

Grayson swore. "You son of a—"

"Couldn't agree more," Russo interrupted. "Brian is Mike's son by his mistress. He had his sister adopt him so they could keep him in the family, without breaking the news about the affair to Mike's wife, so she doesn't know he's a total slimeball. Did I get all that right? Sergeant?"

Jeffries had gone alarmingly pale. "Yes, sir."

Grayson swore. "You idiot. You flat-out told us that Brian was adopted, that we didn't need to test his DNA or look at him as a suspect. But you knew all along he was the killer. The rapist. Didn't you?"

Jeffries violently shook his head. "No, no, no. It's not like that. I swear. I never, in my worst nightmares, thought either of my boys capable of something so vile. I was sure they were both innocent. But I didn't want my wife finding out Brian's real connection to me because of some unnecessary DNA test. I couldn't risk the questions it would raise if the lab questioned why my DNA and Brian's came out looking like father–son instead of uncle–nephew. I figured once you tested the other guys on your list, one of them would match the killer's profile and there'd be no need to test Brian. I wasn't trying to protect a killer. I was trying to protect my wife. Brian knows I'm his dad. But my wife doesn't. I didn't want her hurt."

Grayson narrowed his eyes at him. "You weren't protecting your wife. You were protecting yourself. *You* didn't want to get hurt when your wife left you."

"Enough," Russo said. "We can throw around accusations and blame later. What matters right now is finding Brian Nelson and our missing woman, Nicole Paletta."

Willow's hand tightened on Grayson's arm. "What do you mean *find* Brian? You don't know where he is?"

Once again, Russo glared at Jeffries. "Want to answer that one?"

He twisted his hands together, looking miserable. "Mr. Prescott, the chief told me what you and Willow figured out. That the River Road Rapist may be the one who killed your wife and daughter. I'm so sorry—"

"I don't want to hear how sorry you are. In addition to the DNA lies, you provided an alibi for Brian during my wife's attack. Cut to the chase, Jeffries. Where's Brian?" Grayson bit out.

He swallowed. "I don't know. Truly, I don't. I told him to lay low until the DNA came back on the other suspects. I said I'd tell human resources that he's out sick. He's supposed to come back in a couple of days."

Grayson shook his head, rage warring with disbelief in his expression. "Nicole Paletta is out there somewhere, kidnapped by your son. If you hadn't warned him about the DNA testing, he could have been taken into custody at work today. Instead, thanks to your lies, he's probably doing unspeakable things to her before he kills her and drops off the radar to pop up somewhere else and start raping and killing all over again. How many more will be hurt or killed because you weren't man enough to own up to a stupid affair?"

Jeffries turned ashen. "I'm so sorry."

Russo rapped his knuckles on his desk to get their attention. "We've got a BOLO out on Brian Nelson. Everyone in law enforcement will be on the lookout for him. It's all hands on deck. We're turning over every rock we can to find this guy and rescue Ms. Paletta."

Grayson turned away from Jeffries, effectively dismissing him as beneath his contempt.

"Chief," Willow asked, "have you contacted the phone company, tried to track Brian's cell phone to locate him?"

"We're working with the phone company on that right now."

"I'll get our team to switch gears," Grayson said. "They've been researching five of the original suspects, everyone except Brian. We'll get them digging into his background to try to suggest places where he might hide."

"My team's doing the same. Let's keep each other posted on our progress. Jeffries and his sister will sit down with my detectives and tell us everything they know about Brian, as well. Isn't that right, Sergeant?"

"Yes, sir. Of course, sir. I'll go call her right now, tell her to come to the station." Jeffries rushed from the room.

Grayson and Willow exchanged an uneasy glance.

"Chief," Willow said. "Are you sure you can trust Jeffries not to take off? If he knows where Brian is, he could go warn him."

A slow smile spread across Russo's face, the first he'd had since he'd come into the room. "Like I said earlier today, Detective. You're an excellent investigator. I came to the same conclusion as soon as I spoke to Jeffries about this fiasco. Except I don't think he'd try to warn Brian. He'll want to bring him in himself, to make sure he doesn't get cornered by some other cop and get shot."

"You're tailing your sergeant," Grayson said.

"I've got two of my best guys on it. And a GPS tracker on his car."

Chapter Nineteen

Grayson walked into the converted library the next morning with a tray bearing three coffee cups. "Wake up, sleepyheads."

Ryland didn't stir. He was snoring, facedown across a stack of papers on his desk. Grayson left a cup for him on the far corner, out of the danger zone for flailing arms so Ryland wouldn't knock it over when he woke up. He was betting the smell would wake him soon.

Willow wasn't in much better shape than Ryland. But at least she'd been smart enough to curl up on one of the couches by the front bank of windows instead of falling asleep in a chair.

She opened one bleary eye and held out her hand. "Coffee. Now."

He chuckled. "Sit up first. And maybe next time the whole team works until the wee hours of the morning, you'll take my advice and use one of the guest rooms."

She gulped down half the cup without coming up for air. Her eyes narrowed suspiciously as he stared at her. "What?"

"Your hair. It's, ah, interesting this morning."

"Medusa or windblown goddess?"

"I'll go with windblown goddess."

"Smart man." Her eyes widened. "I have to pee." She shoved the cup in his hand and took off for the bathroom.

Grayson was still chuckling when he heard Ryland yawning. He turned around, sipping from his own cup. "Morning."

"Morning." He yawned again. "Where is everyone?"

"It's Saturday, Ryland. I ordered everyone to head home at about 3:00 a.m. and not to come back for at least eight hours. Although, to be honest, I expect Trent will sneak back long before that. He gave me quite an argument about not wanting to stop working."

Ryland smiled. "Sounds like Trent."

"Hopefully he'll heed my advice anyway. The whole team's running on empty. You all need your rest. I would have made you and Willow go too but you were both already asleep."

Ryland scratched at the five o'clock shadow on his face. "Did they find Paletta? Brian Nelson?"

Grayson settled in a chair one desk over. "Not yet. The police and search teams are working in shifts, doing everything they can. Jeffries hasn't done anything suspicious yet. He brought his sister in to give a statement about Brian, then went home to wait and see if Brian calls him. He hasn't left his house."

Ryland pulled his keyboard toward him.

"It's okay to take a break like everyone else. Go upstairs. Crash on the first bed you find."

"I may in a bit. Just want to check one more thing. I figured Brian will hunker down someplace familiar. People tend to gravitate to places they know, especially in times of stress. With half the county searching for him, he has to be feeling stressed."

"Okay, and…?"

"Well, if I can get someone in the human resources department at Gatlinburg PD to answer a phone on a Saturday, I'd like a copy of Brian's original job application from when he started there, six years ago. I'm hoping it will list the jobs he worked during summers or breaks from college, maybe even some he had in high school. If he worked in a warehouse, for example, maybe if that warehouse is closed down now, out of business, he might use it as a hideout. Or if there's some vacant land near a place he worked before, that could be a place to look too." He held his hands out. "Long shot, I know. But I can't think of much else left to try. And since the police still haven't found him, we might as well go for the long shots."

"Sounds reasonable to me." Willow strode into the room, her hair brushed and looking much closer to the windblown goddess he'd lied about earlier. "If HR doesn't answer the phone, you could call Chief Russo and ask him to rustle up someone to get what you need." She stopped by Ryland's desk. "I'm going to grab something to eat on the run and head outside for some fresh air to get my brain firing again. Anyone want to join me?"

"Maybe. After I make that phone call," Ryland said.

Grayson stood. "Hold on. Both of you. We all want to catch this guy. Me, as much or more than anyone."

Willow gave him a sympathetic look.

"But," he said, "we can't help if we can't function. Eating and sleeping aren't optional. They're a requirement. Even in Special Forces, we tried to make sure we got a full eight hours and a hot meal whenever possible. You work better that way."

"I'm waiting for the punch line somewhere," Willow said.

"The *point* is that you don't need to grab breakfast in a bag. The cook is off today, all the staff is off since it's a weekend. So now I get to cook. Omelets and fresh-baked homemade croissants anyone?"

He headed toward the door, grinning when he heard Willow and Ryland enthusiastically running to catch up.

"NOTHING LIKE SUNSHINE and the smell of roses to clear the cobwebs in your brain." Willow eyed Grayson beside her as they strolled down one of the manicured paths by the gardens. "That amazing breakfast helped too. You know, if you ever get tired of being a gazillionaire businessman, you'd have a great future as a chef."

He chuckled. "I'll keep that in mind."

She pulled him to a stop in front of the last greenhouse, where the path ended and the woods began. "Things have gotten pretty crazy since I told you my theory about Maura maybe being the killer's first victim."

Tiny worry lines crinkled at the corners of his eyes. "They have. You've thought of something else, something that might help the police find Brian?"

"A thread to pull. It may or may not lead anywhere. The thing is, Brian would have still been in college when that happened. A senior, I'm guessing, so around twenty-one or two. If my psychologist friend is right and Brian fixated on Maura, fantasizing about her looks for a while before he got the nerve to approach her, he had to have seen her somewhere on a regular basis. But not so regular that he would have known she'd dyed her hair and cut it. He thought she still had long black hair. Can you think of any way to explain that? Would he have seen her in a grocery store maybe, but she only went there every few weeks and not the week after she changed her hair?"

He leaned back against the greenhouse. "Doubtful. Our cook was in charge of all the grocery shopping. He's picky about his fruits and vegetables. I suppose it's possible she might have gone shopping for clothes or accessories. But she wasn't a fan of the small boutiques we have around here. She liked to go on shopping trips, to Sevierville or Knoxville, places with much bigger stores, more variety."

"Did she go to the same stores all the time?"

"Honestly, I don't know. I can't imagine I'd have charge card receipts going back that far either. But now that I think about it, even if she did, she wouldn't have gone to any of them in the months before her death.

The baby was only a few months old and neither of us wanted to expose her to crowds and the germs that come with them. She didn't even go to her salon that last time she had her hair bleached. They came here."

"They? More than one person? Like, maybe Brian worked in the salon? Wait, that wouldn't make sense. Then he'd know she'd changed her hair. My psychologist friend doesn't think he would have reacted the way he did, chopping at her hair, if he'd known ahead of time she'd changed it. Dang. I was hoping we were on to something."

"You might be," Ryland called out, jogging up to them. He was breathing a little heavily, trying to catch his breath. "The acoustics out here are almost as bad as when the wind snatches your voice at the beach and you can't hear people ten feet away. I was yelling, but neither of you heard me. Maybe it's the trees or the cladding on the greenhouses absorbing the sound."

"Did you find something?" Grayson asked, pointing to the paper in his hand.

"Right. Sorry. It may or may not help but it sure is interesting. This is the previous work experience portion of Brian's job application. He worked *here*."

"Here?" Willow and Grayson both said at the same time.

"Yep. The address he gave is your home address and he listed Mr. Baines as his boss."

"Baines," Grayson said. "The gardens. Brian must have been one of the college kids Mr. Baines hired as temp help. Maura was in these gardens all the time. She spent hours in the greenhouses, cultivating hybrid-roses. That must be where Brian saw her." He swore. "All this time, I thought I'd let her down by not having good enough security at the house, when it should have been the gardens—and the people working there—that I should have guarded her against."

Willow stepped closer to him. "The only way to have protected her from every possible evil person in this world was to lock her away and never let her outside. She'd have been a prisoner in her own home. That's not a life, Grayson. And her death is *not* your fault."

He gave her a crisp nod of thanks, but she wasn't sure he agreed with her.

"What else did you find out, Ryland?" she asked.

He shot Grayson a sympathetic look before continuing. "He listed Baines as a reference, not that anyone at the police station followed up on that. If they had, they might not have hired him."

"Why not?" Grayson asked.

"Because I called Baines and asked him about Brian." His face flushed a light red. "I, ah, hope you don't mind. I wanted to save some time, so I checked the files in your office, figuring you'd have the payroll information there for your household staff so I could get a current phone number for him."

"I'll have to get a lock for that drawer," he said dryly. "What did he tell you?"

"Brian Nelson worked here for three summers. But the last one was cut short, because Mr. Baines fired him. Get this. The main reason was because he was acting inappropriately with some of the female staff. They felt uncomfortable around him."

Willow rubbed her hands up and down her arms. "No surprise there. I felt uncomfortable around him too. There was always something odd about how he'd look at me."

Grayson frowned. "Did he ever hurt you?"

"No, no. I made it clear I wouldn't put up with his unwanted attentions early on."

The worry in his eyes faded and he addressed Ryland. "You said that was the main reason. There was another one?"

"This is the *really* interesting part. Apparently, Brian didn't have much of a work ethic. He goofed off a lot and would disappear for hours at a time. Baines said he'd often see him coming out of the woods after disappearing for a while. When asked, he said he was studying the plants, to help him become a better gardener. Baines said if that were the case, it didn't help. He was terrible."

Willow put her hand on Grayson's sleeve. "This could be it. Maybe Brian had some hideaway out there. And he's still using it even now."

Grayson's expression was less than enthusiastic. "Even if he did, we wouldn't know where to begin looking. These woods cover the back half of the mountain and meet up with the Smoky Mountains National Park on the other side. We're talking thousands of acres of uninhabited land, most of it nearly impossible to hike because the brush is so dense, with steep drop-offs."

"I don't think we have to worry about searching thousands of acres," she said. "Just the ones with something that might provide a good place to hide someone. Something that's close enough to the gardens for relatively easy access, but not so close that someone might accidentally stumble upon it. Some kind of structure, perhaps. Like a fort?"

His eyes widened.

"How far away is it?" she asked.

Ryland glanced back and forth between them. "It? What are we talking about?"

Grayson considered. "Far enough not to hear someone scream. Especially if the acoustics are like Ryland mentioned. He's probably right. I've never thought about that before."

"Uh, guys. Catch me up here?"

Willow hiked her pant leg up, revealing her ankle holster.

"No." Grayson grabbed her wrist as she pulled the gun out. "If anyone goes out there, it's the police."

"Grayson. I *am* the police. Which way to the fort?"

He swore viciously, not letting go of her wrist.

"He could be killing her right now," she argued. "Let me go. Trust me. I know what I'm doing."

"Ah, hell. Ryland, call Chief Russo and tell him there's a fort, an old building in the woods where I used to play as a kid. There's only one room, about twenty-by-twenty, two windows, two doors. It's a hundred yards in from where we're standing, due east through heavy brush. If I remember right, it's about fifty yards south of a creek. Brian Nelson may be using it to hold Paletta hostage, and no telling what else. He needs to get a team up here to thoroughly search the area, but make sure he knows we're out here. If we don't call you, or if we don't come back to this exact spot, in the next fifteen minutes, something's gone wrong. Have Russo send in a tactical team. Hell, send the whole freaking police department."

Ryland took out his cell phone and swiped through his contact list for Chief Russo.

Willow tugged her gun arm free and sprinted toward the woods.

Chapter Twenty

Grayson snatched the gun out of Willow's hand and spun her around, backing her up against a tree.

She stared at him in shock. "How did you do that? I didn't even know you were right behind me."

"Exactly. You didn't hear me, didn't know I was there. I could have snapped your neck and you'd be dead before you hit the ground."

Shock gave way to anger, her green eyes practically flashing sparks at him as she shoved at his chest.

He didn't budge.

"What is this?" she demanded. "Some male chauvinist way of putting me in my place? Telling me women shouldn't be cops or something? That we're the weaker sex?"

"You *are* the weaker sex. It's simple biology, not some chauvinistic insult. Pound for pound, men have more muscle mass. It's how we're built. It sucks, but there it is. Which means you have to be smarter, keep your wits about you and rely on your training. I'd rather have a smart well-trained woman with me on a battlefield any day of the week over some knucklehead brute who's like a bull in a China shop. But what you're doing right now isn't going to help Paletta. It's just going to get one or both of us hurt, or killed."

He handed her gun to her and stepped back, scanning the bushes and trees around them as he did. Lowering his voice, he said, "You don't know this terrain. Neither do I, not anymore. If Brian's using the fort as his base of operations, he's likely been doing it for years. He knows these woods inside and out. Does that police training of yours tell you it makes sense to run in blind in circumstances like this? Because that sure isn't what my army training tells me."

Her face went pale as his words sank in. She glanced around, scanning their surroundings as he'd done. "Okay, okay," she said, keeping her voice low too. "You're right. I shouldn't have taken off like that. But I'm not waiting around for Russo's guys to get here either. Brian could be hurting Paletta right now."

"Agreed. Waiting isn't an option. So we need to work as a team. If you'd waited back there instead of taking off, you'd have heard me tell you to silence your phone like I've done. No one wants to get killed because a text chimed on their phone at the worst possible moment."

She blinked. "Crap. I didn't even think of that." She quickly silenced her phone, then shoved it back in her pocket.

"We need to look out for each other," he said. "Watch each other's backs."

"How? You don't have a gun."

He held up his hands. "I have these. That's all I need."

Her eyes widened.

He checked the compass feature on his watch, then pointed. "Due east is that way. We use hand signals from here on out. Step softly and try to make as little noise as possible. I'll lead—"

"But—"

"*I'll lead.* Maybe it's that male chauvinist thing coming out in me. But I'm not about to let you lead this time. If the killer's out here, I'd rather be the one to run into him first."

Her eyes widened. "Then at least take my gun—"

"Hell, no. I'm not leaving you defenseless. Silence from here on out. All right?"

She cleared her throat. "Fine. Can we go now? *Sir?*"

He nodded, and waited until he'd turned around to smile.

WILLOW FOLLOWED GRAYSON, her embarrassment at going off half-cocked like a rookie overshadowed by her deepening respect for him. During the months they'd worked so hard together to make Unfinished Business a reality, he'd amazed her with his business acumen and ability to juggle that along with his daily conference calls and split-second decision-making for his other companies. But that all seemed inconsequential compared to watching his survival and reconnaissance skills here in the woods.

Even with all those impressive muscles, he could step like a deer, placing his feet in just the right spots to avoid snapping a twig or crunching a dry leaf. And he was constantly on the alert, like a jungle cat sniffing out danger. As an adversary, he'd be mind-numbingly terrifying. She was extremely grateful to have him as an ally. She just hoped she didn't let him down, like making too much noise as she followed behind him or not reacting quickly enough if it came to a gun battle.

She really wished they both had a gun.

He suddenly stopped and held up his hand, signaling her to stop too. She tried to keep her breaths even and quiet as she carefully scanned the nearby trees and bushes like he was doing. A full minute passed before he finally gave the signal that all was well, and they started forward again.

She was getting used to how he operated, so it didn't surprise her the next time he stopped and gave a signal for them to turn. They each rotated in complete circles, her with both hands wrapped around the butt of her gun, ready to fire if Brian suddenly came crashing out of the trees at them.

After what seemed like an eternity later, but was probably closer to five minutes, they stopped and crouched down in the tree line at the edge of a small clearing. She expected to see the fort he'd spoken about, but all she saw was a long mound of dirt about six feet away. Another one was spaced about ten feet from the first, off to the right. Were they burrows? For a raccoon or some other woodland creature? She leaned over, peering between some branches to see the rest of the clearing. This time, she didn't see a dirt mound. Instead, the ground had sunken in, but it was the same shape as the others.

She blinked, and glanced at the mounds again, then realized Grayson was watching her. The grim expression on his face confirmed what she'd just figured out. These weren't animal burrows.

They were graves.

Chapter Twenty-One

Grayson texted Ryland a picture of what he was sure would prove to be graves of some of Brian's victims. Ryland texted back that he would update Russo and that a tactical search team was already on the way, ETA twenty minutes.

Ryland also texted something else, some bad news. Sergeant Jeffries had slipped his tail. The officers assigned to watch him had been worried that they hadn't seen any sign of him for far too long. He hadn't walked past the windows in his house, even though his wife had, several times. So even though his car was still sitting in the driveway, they made the decision to blow their cover and knock on the door.

The panicked look on his wife's face had confirmed their fears even before she let them inside to perform a search. She quickly caved, admitting that Jeffries had snuck out the back of their house a few hours earlier. He'd climbed a neighbor's fence to get away without being seen. But she claimed he'd refused to tell her where he was going or what kind of trouble he was in.

He'd left his cell phone at home and they didn't

know what kind of vehicle he might be driving. If he was going to wherever Brian was, to warn him—which everyone believed—they had no way of tracking him.

The police were going door-to-door, talking to his neighbors to see if anyone had loaned him their car. Hopefully, they'd find out what he was driving, soon, so they could put out a BOLO.

Grayson figured the best-case scenario was that Brian had left Paletta out here but that he wasn't around right now. Unless Brian had built some kind of shelter on his own, which Grayson doubted. Given his penchant for not wanting to work, the fort seemed the most likely place to stash Paletta. If they could find her and get her to safety before Brian returned, it would be far safer for everyone involved.

With Jeffries possibly in the mix though, that added a whole new level of risk. Would Jeffries fire at his former fellow officer, and Grayson, if it meant protecting his son? Or would he do the right thing and take him down? Grayson fervently hoped that Willow wouldn't get to find out.

He motioned her close and whispered the updates. The red spots on her cheeks told him she was furious with her former boss. She probably felt his betrayal even more acutely, since they'd worked so closely together.

Grayson squeezed her hand in solidarity. He understood all too well how critical it was to be able to trust and rely on your fellow soldiers, or in her case, her fellow officers. Even though, technically, she *wasn't* a cop anymore. Her heated declaration earlier about being the police meant she still thought of herself as one.

They circled the clearing, keeping to the cover of the trees. He consulted his compass a few times, making corrections to their course as needed. The ground cover and bushes out here had grown up considerably since he'd been a kid. Maybe because he hadn't been out here, regularly hacking them back with a machete so he could keep a path open to his so-called fort.

The going was slow and difficult, and he worried that no matter how quiet they were trying to be, if Brian was out here, he might already have heard them and was lying in wait.

Which made this little scouting expedition even more dangerous.

If it weren't for the possibility that a woman's life was in imminent danger, he'd pull Willow with him and get her back to safety. He didn't doubt her capabilities, now that she'd calmed down and was using her training. What he doubted was *his* ability to focus without letting his concern for the woman he'd grown to care about making him too cautious, which could be just as dangerous as being too bold and rushing in without assessing the situation.

She jogged to his side and motioned to the right. There, less than fifty feet away, was what they'd been looking for. The fort. It was in better condition than he'd expected after all these years. But then Mr. Baines didn't do anything halfway. He and his precocious employer's son had built it with attention to quality and making sure it would withstand the elements. The siding was gray and weathered, but aside from a few rotting boards near the eaves, it looked sound.

They crouched down, watching and waiting. With no sign of Brian, or Jeffries, they crept through the trees until they were parallel to a sidewall, just out of sight of the open window, should anyone look out. He turned to motion to her to wait here, just in time to see her running out of the trees a few yards down, not stopping until she reached the fort.

He really wanted to swear right now. But at least she was being cautious, ducking down, gun out in front as she eased closer to the window opening. It had been left open, like the doors, probably to provide ventilation.

Since he was left as her wingman, he kept an eye out, scanning left and right, while she carefully eased up to peer through the opening. She ducked back down and nodded.

They'd found Paletta.

Unfortunately, Brian Nelson had found them.

He stepped out of the tree line on their left side, pointing his gun directly at Willow.

Grayson dove out of the trees, dropping and rolling on the ground, purposely drawing Brian's startled attention away from her.

Gunshots rang out as she laid down cover. Brian fired back, but his shots went wild as he sprinted into the woods.

Grayson jumped up and grabbed Willow, lifting her and running even as she continued shooting toward where Brian had disappeared. He skidded around the far corner of the building, out of Brian's sight line.

He set her down, and together they ran through the open doorway into the building. They had to act fast, get the victim out of the danger zone before Brian worked up his nerve to come after them.

The victim's eyes had grown big and round when they ran inside. Her mouth was gagged. Her hands were zip-tied together, as were her ankles. Several more zip ties had been used to connect the ones around her wrists to a metal hook bolted into the floor. She was naked, with dried blood on her breasts and thighs.

Willow swore a thorough list of obscenities about Brian.

Grayson couldn't agree more.

Willow positioned herself by the second door, the one facing the woods where Brian had gone. Grayson ran to the woman and dropped to his knees beside her as he pulled out his pocket knife. She made noises behind the gag, jerking back. Guilt flooded through him as he realized he'd just traumatized her even more. She was shaking and looked absolutely terrified.

"NICOLE PALETTA, RIGHT?" He kept his voice soothing and gentle, as if he had all the time in the world and everything was okay.

She didn't nod or shake her head in response. He wasn't even sure she could see beyond her terror and understand him, but he had to try.

"We're not going to hurt you. We're here to get you out of here. I'm Grayson Prescott. And that's my friend over there, Detective Willow McCray." He didn't figure the lie about Willow still being a cop mattered if it would help put the victim at ease.

Her wide-eyed gaze darted toward Willow, still standing by the doorway.

"I'm going to cut your restraints, okay? I promise I won't hurt you."

Hoping she understood, he quickly sliced through the zip ties, freeing her. She scrambled backward until her back pressed against the wall near the open window.

Grayson wished he had his hands around Brian's neck right now.

"Nicole, help is on the way. The police are sending a team up here to rescue you. But the thing is, we can't wait for them. Officer Willow is protecting us from the man who tied you up, the man who hurt you. But he's going to come back. And we need to get out of here before he does."

She shook her head, her hair flying around her face.

He realized he hadn't taken off her gag. And she seemed too scared or confused to do it herself. "Is it okay if I take that off?" He pointed at her mouth.

She hesitated, then nodded.

Progress.

"Hurry," Willow called out. "I've seen movement out there. I think he's about ready to try something."

Grayson tore the gag off and she started coughing, trying to spit out another piece of cloth stuffed into her mouth. He pulled it out and threw it aside.

"Come on, Nicole. Let's go."

"No, no. You said he's outside." Her voice was raspy and raw, her words barely above a whisper. "Wait here for the police."

"If I thought they could get here in time, we would. The problem is there's no cover in here. Nothing to stop a bullet. Those walls are better than nothing, but not by much. The trees will offer much better protection. It's our best chance."

"He's on the move," Willow called out. The pop of her gun firing sounded, followed by answering gunfire from outside. Then *click*, *click*, *click*.

Grayson jerked around to see Willow running toward him.

"Bad news," she announced as she dropped to her knees beside them. She held up her gun. "I'm out of ammo."

Chapter Twenty-Two

Willow spoke soothingly to Nicole, who was clutching her hand so hard it ached. But Willow wasn't about to tell her that. The poor woman had obviously been through a horrible ordeal.

And it wasn't over yet.

Grayson jogged over to them from the doorway where Willow had been moments earlier. "I don't see him. I think the sneaky little coward may be circling through the woods to get to the other side of the building. We have to get out of here before he reaches it. Meaning right now."

He scooped Nicole up in his arms. She let out a little squeak of terror and started batting at him with her arms.

"Nicole, Nicole, stop," Willow told her. "He's trying to help you."

Grayson shifted her in his arms, ducking his head to the side to avoid a flying fist. "I'm sorry. But there's no time to make this easy on you." He tossed her over his shoulder and he and Willow took off for the same doorway they'd entered earlier.

Grayson swore savagely and they both skidded to a halt in the middle of the building.

Sergeant Jeffries stood in the doorway. And he was raising his gun. Very slowly, Grayson lowered Nicole to the floor, then shoved her behind his back.

"Sergeant, don't. Please," Willow called out, raising her arms as if that could stop a bullet.

But Jeffries didn't point his pistol at her, or Grayson and Nicole, who was timidly peeking around Grayson's side.

He pointed it toward the opposite doorway.

Willow slowly turned. Brian must have stepped inside while their backs were turned. His pistol was pointed at them, as if he'd been about to shoot. But then he slowly turned it toward his father.

"Here to join in on the fun, Dad?" Brian smirked.

Grayson softly nudged his shoe against Willow's, getting her attention. He motioned almost imperceptibly with one of his fingers, toward the back open window. It was plenty big enough for someone to jump through it.

She blinked once, to let him know she understood. Grayson slowly eased back, bumping into Nicole. But she'd been paying attention, and now seemed more than ready to go along with what he had planned, anything to get her to safety.

The three of them started slowly backing up, trying not to make any sudden or obvious movements that might turn either Brian's or his father's attention on them.

Jeffries's face twisted with pain. "Don't talk like

that, son. This isn't you. You don't want to hurt anyone."

"I don't?" Brian motioned toward the woods behind him. "Tell that to all those special gals I've got out there feeding worms." He chuckled.

A keening moan whistled between Jeffries's teeth. He shook his head. "No. No. You're trying to shock me. You wouldn't do something like that. You're not the monster they're saying you are."

He smiled. "You don't think so? I'll bet if you ask Nikki, she might disagree with you." He nodded toward Nicole, who was once again peeking around Grayson. Brian swung his pistol toward them. "Stop right there. Don't take another step."

They stopped. Willow tried to step in front of Grayson, hoping to shield him. He jerked her back, his glare letting her know in no uncertain terms that he wouldn't allow her to do that.

"Leave them alone," Jeffries ordered.

Brian slowly turned his gun back toward his father. "Or what? You're going to shoot your own son?"

"You know I don't want to do that. I want to protect you. I'm here to bring you in. You can't outrun this forever. You need to give up before some gun-happy SWAT guy shoots you."

Brian made a show of looking around. "I don't see any SWAT guys pointing a gun at me. Only you."

"Brian—"

"Shut up. Don't pretend you care about me. I'm your dirty little secret, the one you're too ashamed of to tell your wife about."

"I'm so sorry—"

"Enough. How did you even find me? And why did you bring them with you?"

Jeffries's eyes widened. "I didn't bring them. I went searching for you. When I couldn't find you, I thought maybe you'd head here, to hide out by our favorite fishing hole."

"*Our* favorite fishing hole? The creek out back? The one I brought you to a handful of times in college? It hardly qualifies as *our* favorite spot since you haven't taken me fishing in years."

Jeffries's face reddened and he started blubbering through another apology.

Grayson tugged on Willow's shirt, pulling her with him and Nicole toward the window again. When they reached it, he mouthed one word. "Go."

She glanced at the opening, then back at him, before shaking her head. "Not without you," she mouthed silently.

Nicole tugged on Willow's arm, her eyes pleading with hers.

"I should have paid more attention to you, son," Jeffries continued talking to Brian. "I should have done more things with you. Work's just always so busy and—"

Willow tuned him out. Grayson had just mouthed something else. *Trust me.* The situation was impossible. She was terrified that if she and Nicole jumped through the window opening, they'd be leaving Grayson to die in a hail of gunfire. She instinctively knew he wouldn't dive through with them. He'd want to stay and buy them some time.

He'd asked her to trust him, and she did. He'd been in Special Forces, had fought the enemy overseas and had come back safe and unharmed. She also knew that if he didn't have her and Nicole to worry about, he'd be free to do whatever he was planning, to somehow bring an end to this horrible situation. Although what exactly he planned was beyond her. Trust him. She had to trust him.

She nodded, letting him know she was ready even though the idea of leaving him there was killing her.

Nicole glanced back and forth between them and nodded, letting them know she was ready too.

"Just how did you expect this to end, Dad?" Brian asked, their conversation continuing.

Grayson silently counted down. Three. Two. One. Go.

Willow dove out the window. Grayson shoved Nicole through the opening after her, then disappeared back into the building.

Shouts sounded from inside, followed by a guttural yell. A single gunshot echoed. Willow bit her lip, desperately wanting to know what had just happened, and desperately wanting to help. But she had to do what Grayson wanted her to do. She had to get Nicole to safety.

She grabbed Nicole's arm and yanked her to standing. Nicole wobbled, the adrenaline that had given her strength moments ago seeming to fail her now. Willow grabbed her waist and pulled her arm around her shoulders. Together, they hobbled as fast as they could toward the cover of the trees.

Chapter Twenty-Three

Grayson slowly raised his hands as he stared down the barrel of Brian's gun. He counted himself lucky that Brian was such a lousy shot. But as red as Brian's face was, it was only a matter of time before he pulled the trigger again.

"Don't," Jeffries pleaded. "Please, Brian. Don't shoot. Put your gun down."

"Don't shoot? Are you kidding me, old man? He helped them escape! And he threw a frickin' knife at me!" His knuckles whitened on the grip of the gun. "The only reason I haven't shot again, yet, is because I want to know how he figured out I was here." He motioned with the gun at Grayson. "Does anyone else know?"

"Just Willow and me. We were talking about my childhood and I wanted to show her the fort."

"Fort? What fort?"

"This building. I called it a fort when I was a kid."

Brian rolled his eyes and said something about crazy rich people. He'd bought Grayson's lie about no one else knowing they were here. That would buy some time for Russo's guys to reach this place before Brian bailed. But it didn't do anything to buy Grayson time.

He glanced at Jeffries, who was still pointing his pistol at his son. *Pull the damn trigger.*

Brian snickered. "I heard you were supposed to be some badass Special Forces guy. What happened? You were sick the day they taught knife-throwing class?"

Keep talking, kid. It gives Russo's team more time.

He shrugged. "Maybe I did." He'd have buried that knife in Brian's throat if he hadn't been both trying to shove the victim out the window to safety and whirling around to avoid being shot while pulling his knife out of his pocket. Too bad he didn't have a second knife with him. At least if Brian killed him now, Willow and Paletta were out of the line of fire, hopefully halfway to the safety of his house.

He'd rather give them enough time to make it all the way, to be certain they were out of danger. Keeping Brian talking could buy them that time. And he knew just what to talk about, something that had been eating him alive for over seven years.

"Why did you kill my wife? What did you do with my daughter?"

Brian's face reddened. "I don't want to talk about that."

Grayson clenched his fists in frustration. "At least tell me what you did with my little girl. Is she here? Buried in the ground like the women you murdered?"

Jeffries made a strangled sound in his throat, his face flushed with shame. Was it because he felt terrible about what Brian had done to Maura, to Katrina, to the others? Or because he felt guilty for doing nothing? Even now, all he had to do was pull the trigger to end this. But he still refused to do the right thing.

Grayson shook his head in disgust. The only hope of getting out of this alive was if he took Brian out himself.

The one thing on his side right now was that Brian had moved closer to Grayson after that first shot went wild. He probably didn't want to risk missing his target again. Which meant he was almost close enough for Grayson to jump him. Almost. Grayson needed to edge just a little closer to make sure he could reach him. But he needed to turn Brian's attention elsewhere first. He needed him to focus on Jeffries.

"Sergeant," Grayson said. "Why are you here? The real reason? Are you stalling, trying to get Brian to hang around until backup arrives?"

Brian's gaze darted toward his father. "Did you call the cops?"

Jeffries shook his head, his eyes widening. "No. No, Brian. I wouldn't do that. I told you, I'm here to bring you in myself. I want to protect you so you don't get hurt."

Brian scoffed. "Where was all this tender care when I was growing up? You left me with your stupid sister. Screw it. If the cops are coming, I'm out of here. Just two loose ends to wrap up first." He swung the pistol toward his father.

Grayson darted forward, then lunged.

Bam!

Bam! Bam!

His arms met empty air as he fell to the floor. He rolled and jumped to his feet. Then slowly straightened.

Brian was gone. He must have run out the back doorway, because Ryland stood in the other doorway, pointing a gun where Brian had been moments earlier.

And behind him, in a spreading pool of blood, lay Sergeant Jeffries.

WILLOW SPRINTED THROUGH the back doorway, both hands wrapped around the thick length of wood she'd found, holding it like a baseball bat. She skidded to a stop, shocked and confused at what she saw. Grayson and Ryland were crouched over Jeffries's body, feeling for a pulse, even though it was obvious he couldn't possibly be alive with a wound like that. She looked around, but didn't see anyone else. Had Brian escaped?

Grayson slowly rose to his feet, his gaze riveted on her makeshift weapon. "Willow?" His voice held an odd huskiness to it that was a bit…disconcerting.

"Um, yes, Grayson?"

"What exactly did you plan on doing with that stick?"

She straightened and pitched the wood aside. "Tree branch actually. I was going to hit Brian. Where is he?"

He gave her an incredulous look. "You ran in here, hoping to fight a gunman? With a tree branch?"

Her face heated. "I was trying to save your life."

He swore.

Ryland cleared his throat. "I was just telling Grayson that Trent arrived at the house as I was grabbing my gun from my desk. We ran up here to help and found you struggling to half-carry Paletta through the woods. Trent carried her back to the house while I continued on to the building." He gave her a wounded look. "You promised me you'd follow Trent to the house."

Her face heated even more. "Yes, well, I planned to. But first, I figured I might be able to help even the odds."

"With a tree branch," Grayson gritted out.

She crossed her arms. "You really seem fixated on that. What happened here after I left?"

He turned away, dismissing her. He took the gun from Ryland and shoved it in his pocket. "Did you bring extra magazines?"

"Never thought I'd need extra ammo at your estate. I conceal carry and keep the gun, and the one magazine, locked in my desk while I'm working."

"I'll manage. Did you see which way he went?"

"Guys? What happened?" Willow stopped beside them. She glanced at Jeffries and winced. "Brian shot his own father?"

Ryland nodded. "I was a second too late. Didn't have a clear shot anyway without hitting Grayson. I fired far right to make Brian dive for cover. He ran out the door instead."

"And he's escaping while we're talking," Grayson said. "Which way?"

"North, toward that creek you mentioned."

"All right. Here's what we'll do. When Russo's guys get here—"

"*Grayson.*" Willow put her hands on her hips. "You are not going after Brian. Wait for Russo. Let him handle it."

The skin along his jaw turned white, as if he was clenching his teeth. Without looking at her, he crossed the building and retrieved a knife from the floor. After folding it and putting it in his pocket, he strode back to Willow, finally giving her his full attention, which had her wincing and wishing maybe she'd kept her mouth shut. His expression was hard, like granite, his eyes so dark they were almost black.

"Willow, you could have been killed." His voice was clipped, vibrating with anger. "You shouldn't even be here." He leaned down until his stormy eyes were inches from hers. "*Get off my mountain.*"

She drew back in shock.

He turned his back to her again. "Ryland, get her out of here. Don't let her out of the house until Russo arrives. Have a couple of his guys take her back to her apartment. She doesn't leave until I get there. Understood?"

"Understood. Come on, Willow. Let him do what he needs to do." He grabbed her arm.

"No, stop it." She tried to evade his hold, but Ryland was determined and a whole lot stronger. He half dragged, half carried her out of the building, with Grayson stopping just outside to examine some footprints in the dirt.

"Grayson, don't do it," she called out. "You can't

go after him alone." She looked over her shoulder, as Ryland pulled her toward the woods. "You're a businessman, for crying out loud. Leave this to the police."

He stiffened and slowly turned. "Did you forget the Special Forces part of that equation, Willow? I'm not caught unprepared in an alley this time. I know who I'm after and what they're capable of." He motioned to Ryland. "Go."

Ryland tugged her into the trees.

"Grayson, wait!" She pushed at Ryland and whirled around. "Grayson!"

He'd already disappeared.

Chapter Twenty-Four

"My gun's right there, on my coffee table," Willow argued, aggravated with the two Gatlinburg PD officers currently taking up precious space in her tiny apartment. "Seriously, this is ridiculous. You've checked my minuscule hallway, bathroom, even under my bed. And you searched my closets—*both* of them. Brian Nelson isn't here. He's up on Prescott Mountain with Grayson and half the police force searching for him."

"Kitchen," one of them told the other. "Did you check *all* the cabinets? He's not a huge guy. Pantry. Maybe he's hunkered down, hiding behind some boxes or something." They drew their guns and rounded the peninsula into her kitchen.

"Oh, for Pete's sake," she told them. "A mouse couldn't hide in that so-called pantry. I can barely fit food in there, let alone a person. And you already checked the cabinets."

They searched again, the whole apartment, which took all of twenty seconds. When they came back into the main room, they re-holstered their weapons.

She faced them with hands on hips. "See? There's

no place to hide. I don't even have a balcony and there's no way Brian could crawl up the siding to try to climb through a window. I'm telling you, your boss is being paranoid, sending you here to guard me."

The younger one shook his head. "Russo's not the paranoid one. It's *your* boss, Prescott. Ryland told the chief if something happened to you, Prescott would make his life a living hell."

She threw her hands up. "Come on. Even if Brian could miraculously evade a massive search party and escape, he doesn't have any reason to come after me."

The older officer crossed his arms. "Revenge. From what I hear, you're the one who figured out that Brian's the killer. Maybe he's come to realize that."

The younger one nodded his agreement. "And you're just his type. Long dark hair."

"Okay, that's it. Out. You can guard me from the landing outside my door, or better yet, your car in the parking lot. I've got enough to worry about—namely whether Grayson is safe—without having to deal with tripping over you in my tiny living room. Go."

She shooed them out the door.

"Lock it," one of their muffled voices called through the door.

She rolled her eyes and flipped the deadbolt. Finally, with her audience gone, she could quit trying to appear unaffected and brave. Her shoulders slumped. She plopped onto the couch and clutched a pillow to her chest.

Raw fear, unlike any she'd ever known, coursed through her, making her shake so hard the couch was vibrating. She drew deep breaths, struggling to keep it together. But it was no use. She was a mess, because Grayson was up there on the mountain with a murderer.

She didn't care that he was former Special Forces. That was years ago. And even though he obviously took care of himself, with an amazing body to prove it, that wasn't the same as running dangerous missions every day. The most dangerous thing he faced at the office was a paper cut. How dare he scare her like this and go off hunting a serial killer, with no backup. A sob escaped her and she buried her face in the pillow.

Please be okay, Grayson. Please be okay. You have to come back to me. Please.

She didn't know how long she lay there, but when she finally let go of the pillow, she wasn't shaking anymore. The fear was still there, but she'd managed to get it under control. She let out a long slow breath, then stepped toward the kitchen to get a bottle of water.

"Hello, Willow. *Nice hair.*"

She whirled around. Impossibly, Brian stood in the hallway, his lips curved in a feral grin that had her blood congealing in her veins.

She dove for her gun.

Chapter Twenty-Five

Grayson pulled his Audi into a visitor parking space two buildings down from Willow's apartment, because a police cruiser had taken her usual spot in front of her building. No doubt it was the officers he'd asked Russo to send over to guard her.

He couldn't help smiling as he cut the engine, picturing the feisty argument they'd no doubt have about him ordering her to get off his mountain. She was probably fuming about having the police at her apartment too. It would seem insulting to her to have two police officers guarding her when she was a cop herself, or had been. But just knowing that someone else was there to help keep her safe had given Grayson the peace of mind to focus on the hunt for the killer.

His smile faded. Unfortunately, that killer was still on the run. Grayson had finally had to admit that Brian gave him the slip, no doubt because he knew the woods up there far better than Grayson. He'd been using that fort as his headquarters for years, and the land surrounding Grayson's home as his killing field.

Before Grayson had left, cadaver dogs had already

alerted on the three areas he and Willow had believed to be graves, plus two more. He could only assume that Erin Speck was buried in one of them. No telling how many more they would find. And although it hurt his heart to think about it, one of them very likely could be his daughter's grave. Hopefully, once they captured Brian, he'd finally tell the truth, the whole truth, about that awful day and what exactly had happened to Grayson's family.

He fisted his hands as he got out of the car and started toward Willow's building. Even knowing she was protected, he wouldn't be able to relax until he saw her for himself. He couldn't shake the fear that had taken hold of him when he'd thought of all the times that she'd walked the gardens by his house. Brian could have been out there at the same time, watching her from the woods. Thank God he'd never gone after her. Which was surprising, considering Willow's physical attributes were like a laundry list of features that appealed to an animal like Brian.

He nodded a greeting at one of the yard guys working outside the building he was passing, automatically scanning the man's features to make sure he wasn't Brian in disguise. Willow would probably call him paranoid when he told her about that later. But he was nothing if not cautious. Being in combat did that to a man, had him bracing for danger everywhere he went. So did caring deeply about someone, the way he was only now beginning to realize he cared about Willow.

Russo had Prescott Mountain locked down tight. No one should be able to get in or out without going through a checkpoint. Even Grayson's car had been searched before he'd been allowed to leave. And the mountain was crawling with tactical teams trained for that kind of terrain. On paper, Brian wasn't getting off the mountain unless he was handcuffed or in a body bag.

But Brian was a cop.

He knew what to expect in a situation like this, the standard operating procedures the police would follow. Grayson couldn't help wondering if he'd had a plan B all along, an escape route in case anyone ever discovered him up there. And what worried Grayson the most was that, if Brian was angry enough, he might decide to seek revenge against anyone he felt was responsible for him becoming a hunted man.

Like Willow.

He jogged up the stairs toward the landing outside her apartment. Whether she liked it or not, when he left today, he was taking her with him. To the airport. They were going to hole up somewhere secluded and safe until Brian Nelson was no longer a threat.

When he reached the top of the stairs, he slowed, every muscle in his body going on high alert. There weren't any policemen outside Willow's door and their car parked out front was empty. He couldn't imagine her letting them wait inside. She'd be too keyed up, too annoyed to allow them to hover over her.

He was about to try her door, when he looked down. Two bright red drops of blood stained the wood on the landing. Another drop dotted the wood a little farther away, leading toward her neighbor's apartment.

Chapter Twenty-Six

Willow desperately tried to scream, but the cloth Brian had stuffed in her mouth was held in place by another cloth tied behind her head. All that came out was a muffled sound. She had to let her eyes do the talking, pouring all her hatred and loathing into her glare. Brian chuckled as he checked the zip ties fastening her arms and legs to her bed frame.

"Uh-oh," he said. "This one's a little loose. Wouldn't want you slipping your arm out and punching me right in the middle of our fun." He winked, making bile rise in her throat.

He yanked the zip tie. It bit into her skin, cutting into her. She cursed viciously against the gag.

"Go ahead," he crooned. "I like my girls to fight."

As long as they're tied down and can't fight back.

She wanted so badly to scream and curse at him, to tell him he was nothing more than a coward. She wanted to tell him that he could hurt her, and no doubt kill her, but he'd never conquer her spirit. As long as there was breath in her lungs, blood in her veins, she'd fight with every ounce of strength she had.

How had he managed to escape from Prescott Mountain? From Grayson and the police? There must have been another way out of the woods, a road no one knew about. A way to slip past anyone if they ever found his sick little hideout. She just prayed that he hadn't hurt anyone else during his escape.

Especially Grayson.

He climbed on top of the bed, straddling her. She bucked, hard, trying to throw him off. He retaliated by sitting on her stomach, pinning her in place. His weight squeezed her diaphragm, pressing against lungs already starved for oxygen with the gag blocking most of her airway. She sank back against the bed, conserving precious energy, letting her arms and legs go limp. Drawing in precious air, struggling to draw a breath past the gag with his weight constricting her lungs, suddenly became her only focus.

"There you go. Works every time." He held up a jagged knife, turning it so the metal winked in the light shining down from above her bed. Then, as if he couldn't resist the temptation, he leaned down, down, down, burying his face in her hair. "You smell so good," he whispered against her ear.

She shivered in revulsion.

He laughed and pulled back, once again pressing against her diaphragm.

"In, out. In, out. In, out," he mocked. "Makes you appreciate life, doesn't it? The struggle to breathe?"

Tears ran down her cheeks, and she hated him for it.

He captured one of them on his finger, staring at it as if fascinated. "It's such a shame that I don't have my playhouse anymore." He rolled his fingers where the tear had been, back and forth, back and forth. "I take all the special ones there, the ones worthy of more than a quick screw in an alley. I keep them for a long, long time. So we can…enjoy each other. Over and over again." He leaned down again, his breath hot against her neck, like a rabid dog. "You're one of the special ones, sweet Willow. I had great plans for you. It's a pity we have to speed this up, that I can't keep you, treasure you the way I'd like to."

Nausea roiled inside her. She turned her head to the side, worried she'd throw up and choke on her own vomit.

"I can't stay long. Too many people after me. Thanks to you and your stupid lover." He yanked her hair, making her arch up to relieve the awful pressure. "What should we do in the little time that we have?" he asked as casually as someone asking what she wanted to watch on TV.

Breathe. Breathe. Don't throw up. Breathe.

"Oh, I know. How about I show you what happened to Russo's little foot soldiers? Stupid beat cops who thought they could outsmart me. They were so busy watching the stairs they didn't think to check the other apartment behind them." He arched his brows. "What? You didn't think of that either?" He held up his phone, then started tapping through some menus on the screen. "I must say, your next door neighbor is a real slob. Well, he was a real slob." He turned the phone around, holding the gruesome bloody picture in front of her face.

She screamed against the gag, bucking and jerking, not even caring anymore if it meant wasting precious air. Her lungs seized in her chest. Her eyes widened. She desperately fought for air. Spots swam in her vision, everything going dark.

"Now, now. Can't have you dying on me just yet. We have a lot more to do before that happens." He raised himself up on his knees, still straddling her, but no longer pressing on her belly or chest.

Air rushed in, her lungs finally filling. She nearly wept with relief as she greedily sucked in air through her nose and around the gag.

When her vision cleared, she realized he was stroking her hair, his fingers like claws as he combed them through the long strands, then lifted her hair to his mouth and sucked.

She closed her eyes, determined not to watch whatever else this sick man wanted to do. She was so tired of fighting. She just wanted to let go.

No, what she wanted was Grayson. She wanted to see him one last time, to make sure he could go on without her, that he'd find someone to love. She couldn't bear the thought of him going back to the way he'd been, so closed-off, starved for something as simple as a hug.

"Shall I tell you what I did to your lover?"

Her eyes flew open. *No! Grayson had to be okay. No, please. No.*

Brian rested the flat of the blade on her breast, the cold steel leaving a trail of goose bumps across her skin. He turned the blade, the jagged edge cutting into her skin like fire.

She cried out against the gag.

His eyes danced with laughter as he drew the blade down. Hot liquid trickled down her ribs and sides. "This is the same blade I used on him. I carved Grayson up into little pieces. Starting with his skin. Did you hear that, Willow? I skinned him alive."

"*Liar*."

They both jerked their heads toward the doorway. Grayson swooped down on Brian like an avenging angel, very much alive. He grabbed the wrist holding the knife and jerked it up and back. The knife fell to the mattress. Brian screamed with outrage as Grayson lifted him off her and slammed him to the floor.

Willow bucked and strained against the zip ties, desperately trying to see what was happening on the floor beside the bed. Arms and legs flailed as the sound of fists slamming into flesh filled the room. A solid thunk was followed by another of Brian's screams, this one so pitiful and raw with pain it almost made Willow feel sorry for him. Almost.

A thump sounded. Grayson swore and Brian was suddenly on his feet, cartwheeling around the corner into the little hallway. Grayson was a blur as he jumped up and sprinted after him.

A bloodcurdling scream filled the apartment, followed by a boom and a crashing noise.

"Police, don't move!"

More crashing and thuds echoed from the other room. Willow curled her fingers against the sheets, her body heated with embarrassment at the idea of anyone seeing her there, naked, vulnerable. But more than that, she was terrified that they hadn't gotten there in time. Where was Grayson? Was he okay? She watched the doorway, cold fear making sweat break out all over her body.

Footsteps sounded in the hallway. The familiar figure that suddenly appeared had tears of relief flooding down her cheeks. He was alive. Brian hadn't killed him. Grayson was alive.

"It's okay, sweetheart." His voice was infinitely gentle and soothing. "Everything's okay." He bent over the footrail, slicing through the zip ties on one of her ankles.

She sobbed against the gag.

His tortured gaze shot to hers as he freed her other leg. "It's okay, Willow. It's okay. He can't hurt you now." He quickly freed her from the rest of her restraints, then pulled the cloth from around her head.

She spit out the gag, her chest heaving as she drew her first deep breath in…forever.

"I've got you," he whispered, as he wrapped a blanket around her. Then he scooped her up and carried her out of the bedroom.

Her face heated again when she realized the SWAT team and dozens of her former Gatlinburg PD colleagues were squeezed into her apartment, many of them staring at her as they passed, no doubt wondering what awful things she'd endured.

"Look away, damn it. Give her some privacy." Grayson flipped the edge of the blanket over her head, but not before she saw what was left of Brian Nelson on the floor.

Grayson was right earlier today when he'd told her the only weapon he needed was his hands.

She buried her face against the side of his neck as he carried her outside.

Chapter Twenty-Seven

Willow glanced up from her desk as the library door opened. Ryland and the team began filing in, which meant the celebratory press conference announcing the partnership between law enforcement and Unfinished Business had finally wrapped up.

It had been a month since Brian's rampage of violence had ended on the floor of her apartment. And it had taken every bit of that month for Gatlinburg PD to tie up the loose ends in the investigation. Which had basically put all of the plans for Unfinished Business on hold. But now the company was officially, and publicly, moving forward, finally getting its day in the sun.

Ryland had pressured her to be with them at the press conference. But Grayson had come to her rescue, telling Ryland to respect her decision. Grayson understood, even if the others didn't. Although she was thrilled for all of them, she couldn't stomach the part of the press conference where Chief Russo was going to tell the press the final conclusions of the investigation, including that Sergeant Jeffries had died with honor, in the line of duty.

Russo had done it, partly, to protect the sergeant's family from the vitriol the public would send their way if they knew the truth. But mainly he'd wanted to ensure that Jeffries's widow received survivor's benefits. Noble reasons, sure. But it still rankled for him to be praised like a hero.

Willow supposed there was some validity to Russo's claim that Sergeant Jeffries had died in the line of duty. He'd acted like a cop, confronting the bad guy and trying to save others. And he'd tragically lost his life in the process. But, all told in the final count, after the police dug up half the mountain, fourteen women had lost their lives. And they still didn't know, might never know, what had happened to little Katrina. Her body wasn't found with the others.

One good thing was that fourteen families now had closure, of some type. At least they could bury the bodies of their loved ones, visit a grave someday. Grayson didn't even have that comfort for his little girl.

Nicole Paletta had been rescued, which was another good thing to be grateful about. And there was no denying it was partly due to Jeffries showing up, confronting Brian, distracting him while Grayson helped her escape. But Willow didn't give her former boss much credit for that. He didn't purposely try to distract Brian. His interference, trying to *save* Brian, almost got Grayson killed.

If Jeffries hadn't lied all those years ago, providing Brian with a false alibi during Maura's murder, so many lives would have been saved. And all those women he'd brutally attacked since then wouldn't have had their lives forever changed, or ended, in such a horrible way. Willow's young neighbor would still be alive too, and the police officers assigned to guard her. The damage her former boss's lies had done could never be undone.

But Willow was making an effort to undo the damage, at least in her own life. Although Grayson had encouraged her to stay at his mansion, she'd been determined to go home, to try to get back to her normal routine and banish the images of Brian from her apartment. She didn't want to give him any more control over her life. She didn't want him to win. But too many sleepless nights, jumping at shadows, afraid to even close her eyes, had made her realize that staying in the apartment wasn't the way to win. Living, enjoying life again, was how she would defeat the evil that was Brian.

A few days ago, she'd signed papers to turn in her apartment at the end of the month. And she'd scheduled a moving company to pack everything up and store it, at least until she figured out her next steps. The first step would be packing a bag, today, and heading to a hotel. Then, after that, who knew? Maybe she'd see if that offer of moving in with Grayson was still open.

One of the investigators, Trent, stopped beside her desk, grinning. "Is it true? Did Grayson really tell you, *Get off my mountain*?"

"Grow up." She shoved him, but smiled to let him know she was teasing as he chuckled and retreated to his side of the room.

Grayson had never once brought up that order he'd given her back at the fort. And she had no intention of bringing it up either. He'd done what he felt he needed to do to keep her safe. And she certainly didn't expect an apology for that. Looking back, it was kind of endearing, although she certainly hadn't thought so at the time.

Once the investigators had all returned, she realized that Grayson wasn't with them. She caught Ryland's attention and waved him over.

He perched on the edge of her desk with a friendly smile, as always. Which, of course, made her feel guilty when she thought of all the horrible things she'd said to him as he was dragging her off the mountain. It would be a while before she atoned enough for that and felt comfortable around him again.

"What's up, Willow?" he asked. "You need something?"

"Grayson didn't come back with you from the press conference?"

"He stayed behind to sign the contracts."

"Oh, right. I forgot about that."

"He'll be here soon. He said it wouldn't take more than a few minutes." He stood to return to his desk but she motioned for him to wait.

She scooped the papers she'd been reviewing into a folder. "I have a favor to ask you. And it's a big one."

He glanced at the folder, curiosity lighting his eyes. "You have a new case you want me to work?"

"More like a pet project. It's really important. But

it's…sensitive. I'd rather that Grayson doesn't know about it."

His expression hardened, and his usual smile was nowhere to be seen. "He's my boss. I respect him far too much to hide something from him."

"Believe me. No one holds him in higher esteem than me. I'm not saying I'll never tell him about this… project. Just that we can't tell him right now."

"Willow, I don't—"

"Just hear me out. Let me explain. Then you can decide for yourself whether you agree with my reasoning, and whether you'll help me."

"Fair enough. What have you got?"

She pushed back her chair and stood. "Let's discuss it in the conference room."

Ten minutes later, Ryland was typing furiously at his computer, busily and eagerly working on her *pet project.* Willow smiled her thanks again, but he didn't seem to notice. A true investigator, he was already trying to figure things out and make the puzzle pieces fit.

Willow was grateful that Grayson hadn't come home while she and Ryland were still in the conference room. That would have led to some awkward questions. But as she passed one of the front windows, she saw his Audi parked under the portico. There was no sign of Grayson though. Had he come inside without her realizing it?

She was about to go on the hunt for him when a flash of movement on the far side of the driveway caught her attention. It was Grayson, heading into the woods, disappearing into the tree line.

This wasn't the first time she'd seen him do that. She figured he wanted to stretch his legs, take a stroll in the shade, which was the best place to be if one was outside, as the weather became increasingly warmer. And it didn't surprise her that he was wearing a suit for his walk. She'd still never seen him in a pair of jeans. She smiled. Maybe she could iron out some of the starch in him and teach him to relax someday. If she was lucky enough to have someday with him.

Maybe this was a good time to talk about the future. Her heart swelled with hope as she hurried outside and jogged to catch up. She was ready to take the plunge, to bare her soul, to finally tell him how she felt and pray that he felt the same way.

He'd been achingly patient with her since… Brian. She wasn't ready to talk about what had happened, aside from what she'd had to tell Chief Russo for his investigation. And she hadn't been ready to talk about her and Grayson. She'd felt too fragile, too confused.

But she was stronger now. Not healed, exactly. Maybe she never would be. Trying to sleep through the night without reaching for her gun in a cold sweat was still a problem. But the good memories were coming back, slowly pushing out the bad ones. The memories of Grayson, how gentle and sweet he'd been. How passionately they'd kissed in Russo's office when she was trying to bring him back from his own nightmares of the past.

He'd told her, after that life-altering kiss, that they needed to talk when this was all over. Well, it was over, or as much as it ever would be. And she was ready for that talk.

She sure hoped he was too.

There he was, just up ahead. A little too far for her to call out and be sure he'd hear her. But not so far that she couldn't quickly catch up. He went behind a thick stand of oak trees, spurring her to jog again so she wouldn't lose him.

When she rounded that same group of trees, she stopped so fast she had to grab a sapling to keep from falling down. About ten yards ahead, an elaborate black wrought-iron fence surrounded a small rectangular building. Gorgeous stained-glass windows were set between Greek-style columns. Well-maintained ivy climbed the walls, lending a regal, old-world elegance to the structure. But that didn't hide what it was.

A mausoleum.

And Grayson had just stepped inside.

It must be the Prescott family mausoleum, no doubt housing ancestors of old. And, of course, his wife, Maura. This was a private moment. She shouldn't intrude. But if he turned around and he stepped out in time to see her disappearing into the woods, it would seem like she'd been spying on him. Rather than risk a misunderstanding, she straightened her shoulders and stepped through the open gate.

At the entrance to the building, she saw him standing inside, facing one of the engraved marble squares with his back to her. There were fresh flowers in the vase, those peach greenhouse-raised roses the head gardener had said that Maura was fond of. Although

Willow couldn't read the name beside the vase, she knew it had to be his wife's.

She was just about to step inside when Grayson bowed his head and pressed his palm against the tomb. And that's when she heard him. He spoke Maura's name. He told her that he loved her, that he would always love her, that she would be forever in his heart.

Willow covered her mouth to hold back the sob that wanted to escape. She was such a fool. A stupid fool who'd fallen in love with a man with room in his heart for only one woman—his dead wife.

She quietly backed away, then took off running.

Chapter Twenty-Eight

Willow stuffed another shirt into her travel bag. It had been far too long since she'd hopped on a flight to Kentucky to see her family. And she could really use their love and support right now, more than ever before. Unfortunately, she doubted her mom's famous homemade chicken noodle soup could fix her broken heart. But that didn't mean she wouldn't give it a try.

Her family didn't know what had happened to her here. Russo had promised to do everything he could to keep her name out of the news. And so far, he'd been successful. She didn't want to have her family worry after the fact. She was okay. Or she would be, one day.

Heading into the main room, she took a final glance around to make sure she hadn't forgotten anything that she might need. She was relieved that she'd already arranged for the movers to pack her apartment before getting her heart broken today. It made taking off on an impromptu visit back home much easier. She could really use easy right now.

The only change she'd had to make was a call to the apartment manager a few minutes ago, arranging for him to let the movers in and lock up after they were gone.

She took one last slow walk through her little apartment. She'd been happy here once, with hopes and dreams for her future. It was bittersweet and ironic that this phase of her life was ending, and that those hopes and dreams had completely changed, then died. She was starting over, again, and had no idea what she was going to do next.

Maybe this place could still be a good home for someone else, though, as it once had for her. Anyone looking around wouldn't have a clue about the violence that had happened here. Repairs had been made. A solid wall had been built in the attic by the apartment management, making sure no one could ever cross from one apartment to another as Brian had done. The manager had assured her they were reviewing all of the apartments in the complex to make the same alterations, to keep everyone safe.

Grayson, of course, was the one who'd saved her, twice—at the fort and then here. When he'd arrived at her apartment building that fateful day and saw some blood drops on the landing, he'd known that Brian must already be there. He'd followed the trail to her neighbor's and discovered the bodies of the two officers who'd done nothing but try to protect her. And he'd found her neighbor, right alongside them. She hadn't even known his name and felt guilty now for being so aggravated about all those pizza deliveries.

She squeezed her hands together. Grayson had snapped a picture of the bodies and texted it to Russo, knowing that would bring help faster than even a call to 911. Then he'd gone on the hunt for Brian.

He was a hero. He'd saved her, then held her hand in the emergency room as the doctor treated the cuts on her wrists and ankles, and the path of the knife where it had cut into her chest.

A hot tear slid down her cheek, startling her out of her walk down a scary yet somehow sweet version of memory lane. Grayson had been her hero and she'd always love him for that, even though he couldn't love her back.

For someone who wasn't normally a crier, she'd sure gone through a ridiculous amount of tissues lately. She wiped at her eyes before strapping the travel bag across her shoulder and hip and hurrying to the front door.

She yanked it open, then froze.

A devastatingly handsome man in a charcoal gray suit stood in the opening, his hand raised to knock.

She swore.

Grayson peered at her over the top of his shades as he lowered his hand. "Not what I was going for, but it's a start." He pocketed his shades and motioned toward her bag. "Going somewhere?"

"I'm going to see my family, actually. In Kentucky. A visit is long overdue."

Instead of moving back, he lounged against the door frame, one arm braced on the opposite side, making it impossible for her to escape.

"The sticky note you left on my desk was a bit cryptic," he said. "I was hoping you could explain it to me."

She blew out an exasperated breath and pulled her

bag off and let it drop to the floor. "I don't see how I could have made it any more clear."

"*I quit. Goodbye.* That's all I get? No reason?"

"I didn't know a reason was required."

"Why are you crying?"

She wiped her cheeks, swearing again. "There was a sad movie on TV. It's one of my vices. I cry over the stupidest things."

He arched a brow. "Am I one of those stupid things?"

Her chin wobbled. She crossed her arms, deciding to ignore the tears dripping off her cheeks. "Will you please leave? I have a plane to catch."

"Willow?"

"What?"

He stepped inside and shut the door behind him. "Why did you quit?"

She threw up her hands in frustration. "Maybe I need a change of scenery, okay? Ryland's running everything fine on his own and—"

"I meant why did you quit *us*?" He took a step toward her. "I'd say that maybe I misread you, that my rusty instincts in the relationship department are even rustier than I'd realized. But that kiss we shared before everything went to hell was like a flashing neon sign. I'm pretty sure even I couldn't misread that."

He cocked his head, studying her. "I wanted to give you time to heal, time to come to terms with everything that happened. Did I wait too long? Tell me I'm wrong to think that you want me, that you care about me. Tell me I'm wrong and I'll walk right out that door and never bother you again."

"You're wrong."

He blinked. "Okay. Well. I guess I lied about walking out the door. Because I'm not ready to give up on you, to give up on us."

"There is no us, Grayson." She wiped at her eyes. "There's only you and Maura. That's all there will ever be." She fisted her hands. "I saw you. Earlier today."

He frowned in confusion. "You saw me? Where? Doing what?"

"In the woods. I was looking for you and glanced out the window. You were stepping between some trees just past the driveway. I thought you were going on a walk, stretching your legs. So I decided to join you."

Understanding dawned in his eyes. "You saw me go into the mausoleum."

"I not only saw you, I followed you. I was about to step inside, let you know I was there. But then you started talking…to her. Telling her how much you loved her, crying." She stepped close, until she was almost touching him.

"This probably sounds crazy. But I love you, Grayson. I have for a long time. I'm so totally in love with you that I can hardly breathe sometimes."

His eyes widened.

She lightly pressed her hand against his chest. "I've been hooked on you since that first hug in that obnoxiously loud restaurant downtown. But it doesn't matter." She tapped the spot, just over his heart. "Because there's no room in here for me. There's only room for a ghost. And I can't compete with that."

She started to drop her hand, but he covered it with his, keeping it pressed against his chest.

"To say there's no room in here for you means you didn't stick around to hear everything I said to Maura."

She looked down at the floor. "I heard enough."

"What you probably heard was me telling my wife I loved her, which I do, and always will. I make no apologies for that. If you'd stuck around, you'd have also heard me update her about Brian Nelson, tell her that we'd finally caught the man who'd hurt her, who took our baby girl from us." His throat worked before he continued. "I told her he was evil enough and mean enough to take the knowledge of what happened to Katrina to his grave, that I may never know the truth. But I've made my peace with it, as much as possible anyway."

He drew a deep breath before continuing. "I told her that justice had been served. She could rest in peace and move on." He gently tilted her chin up until she met his gaze. "Then I told her about *you*, Willow."

She stared at him, stunned. "I don't… You told her…about me? Wh-what did you say?"

"I explained that something extraordinary had happened. That I'd closed my heart long ago. But then I met a smart, feisty, beautiful woman who showed me I still had the capacity to love and be loved. This woman gradually worked her way into my heart, my mind, my very soul. She showed me it was okay to take a chance again, that even though there are no guarantees, and there will always be the risk of being hurt, love is worth that risk. This incredible woman showed me how to laugh again, to find joy in the little things. She taught me to *live*."

He cupped her face in his hands, his stormy blue gaze searching hers. "And then I told her the most important part of all. That I'd learned it's possible to find your soul mate twice, because that's what happened to me. I told her goodbye, Willow."

He pressed a whisper-soft kiss against her forehead. "Maura is my past. You're my future, if you'll have me. I love you, and it took almost losing you to figure that out." He smiled. "Timing has never been my superpower." He squeezed her hand on his chest. "This is yours, Willow. It beats for you. I love you with *all* of my heart. Please, please tell me I haven't waited too long to realize that, to see what was right in front of me? Tell me I haven't lost you."

She tugged her hand free and threw her arms around his neck. "You're so much better than chicken noodle soup."

"I don't… Chicken noodle soup?"

"I'm saying your timing is perfect. You're exactly what I need, who I need, right when I needed you the most. Kiss me, Grayson. Kiss me and make these tears go away."

A smile grew like sunshine across his face as he lowered his mouth to hers.

Epilogue

Willow sat on the edge of the bed in their honeymoon suite, watching Grayson with hungry eyes as he toweled off in the bathroom doorway. Never in her deepest fantasies had she ever *really* believed she could call someone like him *hers*. Sexy as hell? Absolutely. A sensual, teasing smile that could make her toes curl with wanting him? The goose bumps on her arms answered that question.

But he was so much more than that.

He was a man who loved deeply, generously and who'd found room in his heart for both of the women in his life—past and present. His love for Maura was a part of him, and always would be. But it didn't diminish his love for Willow. It formed a solid foundation for their love to grow and flourish. And she couldn't wait to see what would happen next as they started a new life together.

Still, as she clutched her phone in her hands, she couldn't settle the butterflies in her stomach. What she was about to tell him was going to change… everything.

His towel hung low on his hips as he padded barefoot into the bedroom. He was heading toward the closet when he stopped in surprise, then veered toward the bed instead.

Leaning over her, he pressed a hungry kiss against her lips, making her sigh as he pulled back. His blatantly male grin told her he'd heard that sigh and knew exactly how smitten she was with him.

"Hey, beautiful. What are you still doing in your nightgown? I thought you wanted to head into town for dinner. Or was there something else you wanted?" He waggled his brows, making her laugh.

"I'm still hungry, for you and for food."

"Well, I can fix one of those problems right now." He winked and reached for his towel.

"Grayson, wait. We need to talk first."

The concern that suddenly filled his eyes had her heart breaking, just a little. He loved her so much and was fiercely protective. Given his past, the terrible losses he'd suffered and what they'd both gone through together, she understood his obsession with keeping her safe. He was still healing, learning to be carefree and not worry all the time. And she was about to throw a curve in front of him, one that was wonderful and bittersweet and frustrating all at the same time.

The mattress sagged as he sat beside her, gently feathering her hair back from her face. "What is it? Do you feel okay?"

She pressed a hand to his chest and leaned into his warmth, selfishly delaying her announcement for a few more precious seconds of just the two of them.

"Willow, sweetheart, you're shaking. What's wrong?" He got down on his knees in front of the bed and started to take her hands in his. He frowned when he realized she was clutching her phone. "Did someone call with bad news? Is your family okay? What is it? Tell me."

To her dismay, tears started flowing down her face.

His eyes widened. "Willow?"

She set the phone aside, and threaded their fingers together. "While you were getting your shower, Ryland called."

He frowned. "Ryland? You're working on our honeymoon?"

"Yes and no. A month ago, when you signed the contracts for Unfinished Business, I asked Ryland for a favor. I wanted him to try to track someone down by working with that forensic genealogist I used on the last case. It was a long shot. I didn't expect anything to come of it, but I had to try. I knew the odds were a million to one that there was even anything to find, but he uploaded the DNA profile from an old case file and got a hit."

He gently rubbed his thumbs across her palms as he listened to her, the worry still there in his wrinkled brow, the crease lines around his eyes. "He got a hit? On what?"

"It's a…missing-persons case. Someone who was missing, presumed dead. For years." She tugged her hands free and cupped his face. "Grayson, it's Katrina. Your daughter. She's *alive*."

He froze, his eyes turning a stormy blue as he stared at her in disbelief.

"It's true," she told him. "She's alive. And she's beautiful and healthy and happy and is growing up in a loving family and—"

"She's alive?" he rasped, barely able to speak.

"She is. We'll never be able to get Brian's side of the story, of course, but from what Ryland was able to piece together, along with what the genealogist found on the ancestry site, we think that Brian may have hurt Katrina by accident and felt guilty about it. None of his other victims were children. But, of course, he wouldn't have wanted to call 911 to get help for her, fearing the police would catch him. So instead, he took Katrina somewhere else."

"What did he do to her?"

The fear in his voice nearly broke her.

"It's a complicated story, but he patched her up as best he could until he got her to a doctor in Missouri. He wouldn't have wanted to take her to anyone in Tennessee who might have heard about Maura and connected the dots. The doctor he took her to worked at a free clinic in an underserved community, the kind of clinic where no one asks for your ID or delves into your past. As the doctor was working to save Katrina, Brian snuck out and left her."

Grayson squeezed his eyes shut, his expression mirroring his pain at hearing his daughter had been hurt, kidnapped, then abandoned.

She took his hands in hers and waited until he looked at her again. "He seems like a kind man, with a successful practice. He and his wife had been trying for a baby for years and had given up. They'd despaired of ever having a child. Then Katrina was left in his care and it must have seemed like the answer to their prayers. He took her in and they raised her as their own. From everything that Ryland's been able to find out, she's had a good life, Grayson. And she's so beautiful. She has Maura's dark hair and your deep blue eyes."

He stared at her in shock. "You've seen her?"

"A picture. Ryland took it this morning, outside, across the street from their home. He just sent it to me with an update on the investigation. It's a little blurry since he was zooming in but—"

"Show me."

She grabbed her phone and brought up the text that Ryland had sent just a few moments ago, then turned it around.

Tears filled Grayson's eyes as he took the phone and held it close, his greedy gaze drinking in every detail. "My little girl. My little girl." He traced the outline of her face, shaking his head in awe.

"Grayson? I know this is a shock. I hope you don't hate me for interfering and—"

"Hate you?" His expression turned incredulous. "I could never hate you, Willow. For any reason."

"Okay, maybe *hate* is the wrong word. It's just, I know this isn't going to be simple. She's over seven years old. She's with the only family she's ever known, or that she remembers. It's going to be complicated and messy and stressful and—"

He pressed a gentle kiss against her lips and set the

phone aside. Then he speared his hands through her hair, his eyes filled with love. And joy.

"Dear sweet Willow. You've given me the best gift a father could ever receive. The knowledge that his child is safe and healthy, and happy. I can do complicated and messy. And don't worry about Katrina. I'm not going to selfishly traumatize her by ripping her from the arms of the only family she's ever known. It wouldn't be fair to her, or the people who've taken care of her all these years. We'll take it a step at a time. Figure it out. Together." He kissed her again, then pulled back, with so much love in his eyes, it stole her breath. "You took a broken man and made him whole. I love you, Willow. I love you so much."

"I love you too. But there's another problem we have to deal with."

His smile dimmed. "What is it?"

"I'm still hungry."

He laughed and squeezed her hands. "Well, we can't have that. I'll hurry and get dressed and—"

"That's not the kind of hunger I was talking about." She tried to waggle her eyebrows, but judging by his laughter, she failed miserably.

That's when he pounced.

They both fell back on the bed, laughing.

* * * * *

Look for the next book in Lena Diaz's
A Tennessee Cold Case miniseries when
Serial Slayer Cold Case
goes on sale in March 2022!

COMING NEXT MONTH FROM

HARLEQUIN

INTRIGUE

#2055 CONARD COUNTY: MISTAKEN IDENTITY

Conard County: The Next Generation • by Rachel Lee

In town to look after her teenage niece, Jasmine Nelson is constantly mistaken for her twin sister, Lily. When threatening letters arrive on Lily's doorstep, ex-soldier and neighbor Adam Ryder immediately steps in to protect Jazz. But will their fragile trust and deepest fears give the stalker a devastating advantage—one impossible to survive?

#2056 HELD HOSTAGE AT WHISKEY GULCH

The Outriders Series • by Elle James

To discover what real life is about, former Delta Force soldier Joseph "Irish" Monahan left the army and didn't plan to need his military skills ever again. But when a masked stalker attempts to murder Tessa Bolton, Irish is assigned as her bodyguard and won't abandon his mission to catch the killer *and* keep Tessa alive.

#2057 SERIAL SLAYER COLD CASE

A Tennessee Cold Case Story • by Lena Diaz

Still haunted by the serial killer she couldn't catch, police detective Bree Clark doesn't hesitate to accept PI Ryland Beck's offer of redemption. The Smoky Mountain Slayer cold case has gone hot again and working together could bring the murderer to justice. But is the culprit the original slayer—or a dangerous copycat?

#2058 MISSING AT FULL MOON MINE

Eagle Mountain: Search for Suspects • by Cindi Myers

Deputy Wes Landry knows he shouldn't get emotionally involved with his assignments. But a missing person case draws him to Rebecca Whitlow. Desperate to find her nephew, she's worried the rock climber has gotten lost...or worse. Something dangerous is happening at Full Moon Mine—and they're about to get caught in the thick of it.

#2059 DEAD GIVEAWAY

Defenders of Battle Mountain • by Nichole Severn

Deputy Easton Ford left Battle Mountain—and the woman who broke his heart—behind for good. Now his ex-fiancée, District Attorney Genevieve Alexander, is targeted by a killer, and he's the only man she trusts to protect her. But will his past secrets get them both killed?

#2060 MUSTANG CREEK MANHUNT

by Janice Kay Johnson

When his ex, Melinda McIntosh, is targeted by a paroled criminal, Sheriff Boyd Chaney refuses to let the stubborn officer be next on the murderer's revenge list. Officers and their loved ones are being murdered and the danger is closing in. But will their resurrected partnership be enough to keep them safe?

Still haunted by the serial killer she couldn't catch, police detective Bree Clark doesn't hesitate to accept PI Ryland Beck's offer of redemption. The Smoky Mountain Slayer cold case has gone hot again and working together could bring the murderer to justice. But is the culprit the original slayer—or a dangerous copycat?

Read on for a sneak preview of
Serial Slayer Cold Case,
part of A Tennessee Cold Case Story series,
from Lena Diaz.

Chapter One

Maintaining a white-knuckle grip on the steering wheel while negotiating the treacherous curves up Prescott Mountain on his daily commute was typical for Ryland Beck. *Smiling* while he resolutely refused to look toward the steep drop on the other side of the road *wasn't* typical. Nothing, not even his phobia of heights, could dampen his enthusiasm this chilly October morning. Today he'd begin his investigation into a serial killer case that had gone cold over four years ago.

Bringing down the Smoky Mountain Slayer was the challenge of a lifetime. No suspects. No DNA. No viable behavioral profile. In spite of the lack of evidence, Ryland was determined to put the killer behind bars. He wanted to give the families of the five victims the answers and justice they deserved.

Unfortunately, what he couldn't give them was closure. Closure, as he well knew, was a fictional construct. The death of

HIEXP0122B

a loved one would always leave a gaping hole in the hearts and lives of those left behind. But knowing the victim's murderer had been caught and punished would go a long way toward making the excruciating grief more bearable.

He continued winding his way up the mountain toward UB headquarters as he considered the limited information he'd found on the internet about the killings. The Slayer's modus operandi was consistent: all of his victims were strangled, their bodies dumped in the woods in Monroe County. But aside from them being young women, the victimology was all over the place. Their educational and economic backgrounds varied, as did their ethnicity. Some were married, some weren't. Some had children, some didn't. All of that made it nearly impossible to build a useful profile to help figure out who'd murdered them.

The detectives from the Monroe County Sheriff's Office had deemed the case unsolvable. But here in Gatlinburg, Ryland had a unique advantage: an über-wealthy boss who knew firsthand the suffering a victim's family endured when a murder case went cold.

Seven years after his wife was killed and his infant daughter went missing, Grayson Prescott had given up on the stagnant police investigation. He decided to create a cold case company called Unfinished Business. Just a few months later, UB had solved the case. Now, the thirty-three counties of the East Tennessee region had formed a partnership with UB and were clamoring for them to work their cold cases.